POSITIVELY SPEAKING

INSIGHTS AND STORIES TO IGNITE YOUR LIFE

LOU STOOPS

SIMON & SCHUSTER

Printed in the United States of America

10 9 8 7 6 5 4 3 2 1

Please visit our website at www.sscp.com

ISBN 0–536–01878–2

BA 98634

SIMON & SCHUSTER
160 Gould Street/Needham Heights, MA 02494
Simon & Schuster Education Group

"Unprovided with original learning, unformed in the habits of thinking, unskilled in the arts of composition, I resolve to write a book."

—Edward Gibbon

Dedicated to Two Incredible Women and Three Great Children

Delia Irene Stoops
My mother for giving me life and unconditional love.

Cynthia Sanderson Stoops
My Wonderful Wife; My Soul-mate

Elizabeth, Jonathan and Joanna
You three are my legacy.

Thank Yous

Russell & Loretta Sanderson
For giving me my beloved wife.

Vickie Lawson
My secretary and my friend. Thanks for the encouragement and assistance.

Derek Clay
For giving me my first opportunity to make *"Positively Speaking"* available to people.

To the Seerley Creek Christian Church
A kind and caring community of faith that I have been blessed to be a part of.

David Daniels
A special thanks to David, who made this book possible.

Foreword

It is difficult to imagine a more treacherous time for idealism and vision. We can argue that the mid 20th century presented its own horrors to hope with the violence of world war. As terrible as global conflict—with its incalculable suffering and anguish—was, it was seen as a struggle where forces of good and evil, right and wrong were clearly defined. Today the demons may be less obvious. Yes, there is still warfare, hatred, hostilities and other forces of darkness which rip at the human fabric. What makes this time uniquely vulnerable is the way that negativity plays its hand. Terrorism, a cowardly way to make war, lurks just out of view sowing seeds of despair. Public leaders betray trust and demonstrate, while they have feet of clay, they are also empty vessels, void of character and ideal. Media images are cynically tuned to create false impressions and destructively designed to create contrived desires. Children can't be just children, they must be consumers to be sold to. Men and women can't be just who they are, they too must be consumers to be pitched to. In the age of the modern media where fabricated reality is used to sell, concepts of self, attitudes of worth, sexual roles and general human values are disturbed. The result of modern life can leave us wondering who we are, what has value and worrying about how we can cope. Our efforts to survive leave us looking for navigational help.

Lou Stoops, in *Positively Speaking*, cultivates what I believe is our instinctive reach for the ideal and he does so in a way which provides a vision. We need to build up the structure of the human spirit. We have work to do to spread wisdom and clarity and illumination. Lou speaks to us in a way which reaches that part of the human being which has in all ages led this species to accomplishment, to overcoming, to a spirit and state of well being. Lou speaks to us with a voice that has been tempered by pastoring, by counseling, by teaching and serving. He has looked into faces of pain and grief and he has learned to discern hope. He is a realist who understands that idealism is a tool which God has ordained to help humankind change the world, often beginning with ourselves. This is a time and age which needs to hear the message from our contemporary apostles of hope.

It is strange to think that the once distant and futuristic 21st Century will be defined and settled by us, children of the 20th Century. We are the future's first inhabitants. *Positively Speaking* is a message which can help us live now and live even better in the future. It is a navigational aid on our path to a more positive life.

Tom Cochrun
Television Producer, Author of *The Sanibel Arcanum*

Contents

Chapter One

1

Giving

Go for It, Get It, Give It

"His deeds are his monument, his life is our inspiration."

So reads the inscription on the base of the statue of Milton Hershey, with his arm around a young boy. Why such a statue? Well, simply put, he deserved it.

When he was a young boy of fifteen, Milton Hershey got a job as an apprentice to an established candy maker. Working hard and saving his money, after four years, Milton was able to open his own candy store. He had attained the prize of dreaming the American dream. But as all business owners can testify, to maintain a business takes even more effort than was expanded to create it. The long hours and hard work took a toll on Milton's health. He had to close his dream.

After regaining his strength, he moved to New York City, getting a job delivering candy by horse and wagon to the customers of his employer. It wasn't long until circumstance reared its ugly head. Actually the horse spooked and the wagon dumped the inventory. Old Milton was fired.

He decided he would go back to his home in Lancaster, Pennsylvania. He again worked hard but candy was in his veins. He rented an old abandoned factory and began to produce caramels and then chocolates. When new machinery came into existence, he was able not only to refine his product, but mass produce it as well.

The year was 1903. Milton was forty-six. He built a new factory and became a millionaire. Milton Hershey had made it. The American Dream was now firmly his. He had persevered, refusing to quit. In spite of his struggles, he stayed true to his passion. As encouraging as his story is, there's much more to Hershey's life than making money and attaining a dream.

When Milton was a boy, his parents had taught him well. Their words rang out throughout his life. "The surest road to success is to lose yourself in service to others." Milton Hershey lived by that creed.

His business succeeded and so, he set about reaching out. He built an entire town for his employees to live in. He constructed houses, stores, schools, hotels, city services, parks and even a zoo!

He and his wife loved children but could never have any of their own. In 1910, they opened a school and shelter for boys. It became known as Hershey Industrial School. At the school, boys could learn a trade. Upon graduation, each boy received one hundred dollars to start out in life. Over the years, thousands of young men have been given a head start because of the generosity of Milton Hershey.

It's not just the dream of money, fame or some other worldly attainment that fuels the drive of men and women for achievement. It's the quest for meaning.

When Hershey died in 1945, he left the bulk of his vast fortune to continue the work of service he had devoted himself to. Over the years the school has been renamed the Milton Hershey School, and girls have become a part of the mission as well. Over twelve hundred students a year are educated as a result of Milton's vision for service.

It's not just the dream of money, fame or some other worldly attainment that fuels the drive of men and women for achievement. It's the quest for meaning. Service brings meaning to our lives. When all is said and done, it's our service to others that will be remembered.

Show Me the Money

Too many Americans define success purely in monetary terms. Making money, having money and spending money become the goal. Believe me when I say that money is an inadequate definition of what it means to be successful. Don't misunderstand me here. I'm not against having money. Having money is good as long as money doesn't have you!

Successful people use money as a tool to benefit themselves and others. To fall in love with money leads to disaster. Consider the words of King Solomon of ancient Israel, "Whoever loves money never has money enough; whoever loves wealth is never satisfied with his income."

People who lust for wealth and believe it to be the benchmark of success set themselves up for misery. Wealth is fleeting and shouldn't be considered as the ultimate measure of our achievements.

In 1923, a group of the world's wealthiest men gathered at the Edgewater Beach Hotel in Chicago, Illinois. At that time, those men controlled more money than was contained in the United States Treasury! The following is a list of those who were there and how they ended up:

- Charles Schwab—president of the largest independent steel company—died broke.
- Arthur Cutten—greatest of the wheat speculators—died abroad, insolvent.
- Richard Witney—president of the New York Stock Exchange—died just after release from Sing Sing Prison.
- Jess Livermore—greatest "bear" on Wall Street—committed suicide.

- Leon Fraser—president of the Bank of International Settlements—committed suicide.
- Ivar Krenger—head of the world's greatest monopoly—committed suicide.

That success and money are not synonymous can be seen in the words of Greek millionaire Aristotle Onassis, who said, " . . . after you reach a certain point, money becomes unimportant. What matters is success."

When it comes to money, I like what John Wesley advised,

> Make all you can.
> Save all you can.
> Give all you can.

Being successful is being a giver; can there really be any other reason for living than the realization that we're here to be of benefit and to bring glory to our Creator?

Hoarders aren't successful; Givers are. Jesus said, "It's more blessed to give than to receive." Givers enjoy more than those who live only for themselves. In fact, Karl Menninger, psychiatrist, author and primary founder of the Menninger Foundation, said, "Generous people are rarely mentally ill people."

In life, all that glitters isn't gold; live for significance and you'll be successful.

The Blessing Is in the Giving

"When it comes to giving, some people stop at nothing."

That quip uttered by an unknown individual sums up the generosity threshold of many in our consumption-oriented society. We often seem more concerned with what we can get rather than what we can give.

The greatest achievements are realized through the selfless efforts of people who choose to give. To do great things requires an expenditure of time and energy that brings little immediate reward.

Those who've pioneered in the sciences have labored to bring a resolution to big problems only to have many of their experiments fail. Yet, their failures contribute to the ultimate resolution as others build on what they've done.

Being successful is being a giver; can there really be any other reason for living than the realization that we're here to be of benefit and to bring glory to our Creator?

To give purely, we must possess a selfless attitude. We give because we choose to.

Giving must become a way of life if significance is to be experienced. We've got to see our efforts to better others as meaningful, and not be concerned when we don't instantly profit.

Some do good with the expectation of a "thank you." If they fail to receive what they've determined to be their due payment, they become disgruntled and dismayed. Motivation behind giving is as important as giving.

To give purely, we must possess a selfless attitude. We give because we choose to. Jesus said, "It is better to give than to receive." The reward for giving is in the action of giving. Even if we have little, we can give big, if our hearts are big in love and concern.

I like the story of a man by the name of Mr. Roth. It first appeared in a 1990 edition of Leadership magazine. It's not known who wrote it, but it tells a wonderful "giving" story.

"An old man showed up at the back door of the house we were renting. Opening the door a few cautious inches, we saw his eyes were glassy and his furrowed face glistened with silver stubble. He clutched a wicker basket holding a few unappealing vegetables. He bid us good morning and offered his produce for sale. We were uneasy enough to make a quick purchase to alleviate both our pity and our fear.

"To our chagrin, he returned the next week, introducing himself as Mr. Roth, the man who lived in the shack down the road. As our fears subsided, we got close enough to realize that it wasn't alcohol, but cataracts, that marbleized his eyes. On subsequent visits, he would shuffle in, wearing two mismatched right shoes, and pull out a harmonica. With glazed eyes set on a future glory, he'd puff out old gospel tunes between conversations about vegetables and religion.

"On one visit, he exclaimed, 'The Lord is so good! I came out of my shack this morning and found a bag full of shoes and clothing on my porch.'

"'That's wonderful, Mr. Roth,' we said. 'We're happy for you.'

"'You know what's even more wonderful?' he asked. 'Just yesterday, I met some people that could use them.'"

You can be poor in material things but rich in heart. Unless you give though, the heart-wealth evaporates.

To be a real achiever, having a genuinely significant life, make the decision to be a selfless giver. The reward will be in the giving.

Chapter Two

Focus

Junk or Jewel?

Our lives are a lot like money. We can invest ourselves or squander ourselves. Life can be wasted or put to work to bring real profit. It really is about the purpose we have that determines the return on our life. Let me illustrate:

An object becomes more valuable when used for lofty purposes. Some years ago I ran across this insight about purpose and value:

Consider an old bar of iron in a junkyard. Its worth is about five dollars in its raw form. But when used in progressive ways, it becomes more valuable.

- Horseshoes—$10
- Steam engine—$23
- Mould-board for a plow—$50
- Scissors—$83
- Needles—$8,300
- Surgical instruments—$33,000
- Balance spring for watches—$166,000

Having a valuable purpose contributes to having a valuable life.

We all know that a lofty purpose doesn't just happen, it requires a certain amount of introspective thought. Too many people just sit around and wait for something to happen. "Sitting around" gets you nowhere.

Thomas Carlyle once said, "A man without a purpose is like a ship without a rudder—a waif, a nothing, a no man. Have a purpose in life, and, having it, throw such strength of mind and muscle into your work as God has given you."

Value comes as a result of purpose because purpose acts like a laser beam. An intense focus of energy and effort that results in attainment.

Some years ago Yogi Berra, the famous catcher for the New York Yankees, was playing against the Milwaukee Braves. Hank Aaron, the Braves' great power hitter, was up to bat. It was a World Series game. Berra was making noise, the chatter that's designed to distract the batter. He told Aaron, "Henry, you're supposed to hold it so you can read the trademark."

Aaron ignored Berra, choosing to hit the ball into the left-field bleachers. As he completed rounding the bases, he looked Berra straight in the eyes and said, "I didn't come up here to read."

Too many people just sit around and wait for something to happen. "Sitting around" gets you nowhere.

Purpose brings focus; focus brings effort; effort brings attainment and attainment of worthwhile ends brings value. Don't just spend yourself, make a meaningful investment.

Just Getting By?

"I can't imagine a person becoming a success who doesn't give this game of life everything he's got.

Walter Cronkite

Far too many people, as well as companies, are content to just get by. They do no more than the minimum and wonder why they aren't receiving better results. But consider this, if you determined that 99.9% was good enough, then:

- 22,000 checks will be deducted from the wrong bank accounts in the next 60 minutes.
- 268,500 defective tires will be shipped this year.
- 291 pacemaker operations will be performed incorrectly this year.
- 18,322 pieces of mail will be mishandled in the next hour.
- 12 babies will be given to the wrong parents every day.

Of course, it becomes quite clear that good enough isn't really good enough.

If you're going to excel at what you do, you've got to give extra effort and not be content with what many accept as all right.

Theodore Roosevelt once said, "When you play, play with all your might, but when you work, don't play at all. No man can hope to be outstandingly successful at anything unless he exerts the effort to run an extra undemanded mile."

Giving more than you're required paves the way for greater opportunity. Reputation is built upon excellence and commitment. By providing wholehearted service, the individual or the company stands out as a valuable asset.

By doing more than is expected, by giving over-the-top effort, the creation of great things is possible. During the Crimean War, a young woman was moved with compassion at the horrid loss of life and severity of the wounds. She would walk among the injured and tend to those

If you're going to excel at what you do, you've got to give extra effort and not be content with what many accept as all right.

suffering in agony. Florence Nightingale did more than was expected and her efforts helped establish the nursing profession. Such is the result of going the extra mile.

Don't be content to just get by. Make an extra effort in the job you have now and anticipate your horizons expanding.

You can't arrive at achievement if you're wandering aimlessly.

Know Where You're Going

Are you on the right track? Do you know where you're going? Are you sure? Well, it's important to know if you're going to make progress, and attain the prize. You can't arrive at achievement if you're wandering aimlessly. Ralph Waldo Emerson once said, "The world will always make room for the man who knows where he's going."

Being successful in any enterprise requires a concerted effort of concentration on a specific goal; to single-mindedly pursue a predetermined destination until arrival. Too many people live scattered lives. They're preoccupied with so many concerns that they have little energy to sort out what needs to be done to get to the next level.

This disjointed and distorted approach to life is not limited just to the individual. Companies often subscribe to this same pointless philosophy.

The lack of long-term direction, which is often sacrificed for short-term gain, causes many a business to falter and often fail. The individual and the company would be better served, to determine where they want to be over the long haul and then establish a strategy to get there. Success is a step-by-step process.

Walter Cronkite said, "I'm convinced that the real secret of success is to keep your eye on the road immediately ahead." That philosophy only contributes to success when you've determined where you want that road to end up.

Andrew Carnegie, one of the all-time great captains of industry, observed that many business endeavors fail because they move out in too many directions, never mastering one. He said, "Here is the prime condition of success, the great secret. Concentrate your energy, thought and capital exclusively upon the business in which you are engaged. Having begun in one line, resolve to fight it out on that line, to lead in it, adopt every improvement, have the best machinery and know the most about it."

He went on to say, "The concerns which fail are those which have scattered their capital, which means that they have scattered their brains also. They have investments in this, or that, or the others, here, there and everywhere. 'Don't put all your eggs in one basket' is all wrong. I tell you, 'Put all your eggs in one basket, and then watch that basket, day and night.' Look around you and take notice. Men who do that do not often fail. It is easy to watch and carry one basket. It is trying to carry too many baskets that breaks most eggs in this country. He who carries three baskets must put one on his head, which is apt to tumble and trip him up. One fault of the American businessman is lack of concentration."

Are you on the right track? Do you know where you're going? You need to be sure. Find out what you want to do and do it. Determine where you want to go and get on the right road that will take you there. Let the journey begin now.

Simple, But Not Easy

You know, the greatest achievements in life are possible when we determine to do some very simple things. One of the simplest things we can do that can guarantee achievement is to set goals. Too simple? No, not really. Goals require decision and action and yet, it's something we all can do.

Setting goals gives us targets to aim for. When we write goals down, we increase our probability of achieving them. By daily reviewing them, we saturate our minds and that has a very powerful way of working itself out in what we do.

Far too many people drift through life and some even boast that they never set goals. It seems to those folk that goals tend to restrict and remove the spontaneity of living. To the contrary, goal setting is extremely freeing in that knowing the direction you're heading towards allows for progress to be observed and additional time to be spontaneous because you're unencumbered by the many tangents that drifting creates.

Bernard Baruch's life speaks well of the value of setting goals. He was raised in orphanages but would later work his way through school until graduating in 1889 from The College of the City of New York.

Baruch was an intelligent man and shrewd in business. He made a fortune through investments and was a member of the New York Stock Exchange. He was sought after for his counsel and served seven presidents as an economic advisor. He held many government positions over the course of his life.

Baruch was also known as the "park bench philosopher." He was famous for holding conferences on park benches for large crowds in New York City and Washington, D.C.

Upon being asked how he had achieved such a rags to riches life, he simply replied, "I learned from the magnifying glass." He went on to say, "I saw the sun's rays fall on everyone. But the magnifying glass captures the sun's rays, harnesses its power, focuses its energy, and brings forth fire."

You see, all of us can achieve but many don't. Setting goals magnifies our energy; it gives us focus and allows for the maximum force to be applied to our endeavors. When we are goal oriented we are on our way to meaningful results.

What is it that you'd love to accomplish in your life? Are you wishing or are you working? Are you drifting or are you determining? You can begin to achieve today if you will just take the time to write down your goals and begin. Remember the magnifying glass. It's that simple!

Hang On to the Dream

Sometimes you must do what doesn't seem reasonable; you must risk in order to build something that will be uniquely yours. Akio Morita was just that sort of man. In his book, *Made In Japan*, he relates how he turned down a deal that seemed to be just what his fledgling company needed.

Morita was co-founder of the Sony Corporation. In the early years of his company, the corporate giant Bulova offered to purchase 100,000 units of Sony's transistor radios. At that time, Sony was only moving about 10,000 units a month and this deal with Bulova would have propelled the fortunes of Sony.

After much thought, Morita declined their offer. The deal was worth more than ten times Sony's value at the time! Morita's associates thought he was crazy. Why would he not have jumped at the extraordinary opportunity to put Sony on the map? Why wouldn't he make the move that would flood Sony's pockets with positive cash flow? Well, Morita had a dream.

Bulova had wanted Sony's radios but they intended to put their own name on them. Morita didn't like that. He didn't want to build Bulova's

Remember the magnifying glass.

A lot is lost in life because we fail to employ patience in our pursuits. . . . If you want to benefit from your endeavors, look to the long run.

name, he wanted to build Sony. He wrote to startled Bulova executives, "Fifty years from now my company's name will be as big as yours, and I know that the radio I've created is going to help us develop that name." Wow! That was a man who didn't jump for the immediate gain, but focused upon the long-term dream.

A lot is lost in life because we fail to employ patience in our pursuits. We jump for immediate short-term results at the expense of long-term achievement. If you want to benefit from your endeavors, look to the long run. Don't jump too soon. You may have to do some things that don't seem reasonable to others. That's all right. It didn't hurt Akio Morita.

Quit Is a Four-Letter Word

When you've set your sight on success, it's important to remind yourself that it won't be easy. Nothing worthwhile in life ever really is. If you want a bountiful garden, you're going to have to work for it. There's soil preparation, planting, fertilizing, watering and weeding. Only when you do what's necessary, can you hope to see a harvest. The same is true in all our valuable pursuits.

In our culture, "easy" is a religion. People really believe that they can win with little or no effort. This mindset profits countless companies that promote easy solutions for problems ranging from weight loss to money making. *Easy* is what sells the lottery; *easy* is how advertisers clothe every product; *easy* drives the American economy. Easy, however, isn't reality, and when people find that out they become discouraged. That leads many to *quit* when attempting to succeed, often just short of victory.

Success is often a matter of doing the right things the right way right now and not quitting until you arrive at the right outcome. Quitting is an option you can't afford. The reward often comes two minutes until too late.

The lack of immediate success isn't a reason to quit. If you quit because things aren't easy, you may be cheating yourself of the dream you've been working toward.

When you want to quit, here are some things to consider:

- Though you've had difficulty, you've also learned a lot. Your tough experiences have made you more likely to succeed.

- Quitting now throws away all that you have sacrificed up to this point.
- Quitting now not only affects you, but also those who've been counting on you.

The individual that plows, plants, fertilizes, waters, and weeds, loses all if they go out and dig everything up without giving enough time for the harvest to take place. Quitting is not giving yourself enough time for success. Anybody can quit and most do, but winners keep plugging along.

When things get tough, just remember that success isn't easy and takes time and effort. Jacob Riis learned this truth and made the following observation, "When nothing seems to help, I go and look at a stonecutter, hammering away at his rock, perhaps a hundred times without as much as a crack showing in it. Yet at the hundred and first blow it will split in two, and I know it was not that blow that did it—but all that had gone before."

Go ahead and set your sights on success. Know that it won't be easy and don't quit when it gets tough.

See It!

Having goals is about seeing where you want to go. If we can't see ourselves making progress toward a designated destination, we will lack the resolve required to press on.

Florence Chadwick waded into the water off Catalina Island. It was a foggy day, July 4th, 1952, and Florence had hoped to swim the channel from the island to the California coast.

She was no novice to long distance swimming. She had been the first woman to have successfully swum the English Channel. She had done so in both directions!

On that day in July, the water was cold and the fog was thick. Even seeing the boats that would accompany her was a difficult task. She entered the water with determination and began the long swim. For fifteen hours she would labor toward the finish, but to no avail. She decided to quit. Her trainer encouraged her to keep going but since she couldn't see because of the fog, she decided not to go on. The fog had gotten the best of Florence, with only one mile left to swim.

Success is often a matter of doing the right things the right way right now and not quitting until you arrive at the right outcome.

She later said, "I'm not excusing myself, but if I could have seen the land I might have made it." She didn't complete the swim because she couldn't see the goal.

Florence Chadwick would reach the goal, however. Two months after her failure, she again set out to swim the channel. Because she could see the goal, she not only swam the distance but set a new speed record as well.

The importance of goals lies in our being able to see an end in sight. We need a benchmark. Goals provide that and more. Goals give us a sense of mission. General George Patton thought so much of goals that give mission that he would often ask soldiers, "What is your mission?" He thought that the ability to articulate their mission was the most important piece of information a soldier could carry into battle.

True enough. If you're ever going to fight the good fight in life, you certainly must know which way to go. Set goals so you'll see where you want to end up in life.

If you're ever going to fight the good fight in life, you certainly must know which way to go.

Chapter Three

Attitude

Is Abuse Your Excuse?

He's written over four thousand songs, is the author of numerous books, Broadway plays, pioneered the talk show format in television, and is an accomplished jazz pianist. Though his accomplishments are many and successful is how he's viewed, it wasn't always so.

As a boy he lived in Harlem, New York. His parents were vaudevillians and often traveled extensively. His mother, when home, was an abusive woman, that for some reason, chose him as the object of all her pent-up wrath.

He went to eighteen different schools and was shuffled around to numerous alcoholic aunts and uncles. When he was thirteen years old, he ran away from home. He had decided to live with an aunt in California, and rode his bicycle most of the way until it broke down. He rode freight trains the rest of the way, eating the ant-infested scraps hobos left behind.

When he was old enough, he joined the army. Eventually, he got into radio and then on to television. **Steve Allen** is best known for creating *The Tonight Show* in 1954.

I've always considered Steve Allen a real Renaissance Man. His harsh experiences as a child could have very easily destroyed him. Instead he responded to his pain in a positive, creative fashion. He became better instead of bitter.

All of us struggle with our own pain; most of us have had our share of hurt and could recite the wrongs that have visited us. Yet, to live positively we must get beyond the pain of the past and embrace the possibilities of the moment, allowing us to create a future!

Do It Anyway

"The men who set out to do what others say cannot be done are the ones who make the discoveries, produce the inventions and move the world ahead. Believing in success can help make it so."

T.J. Watson Jr., IBM

There's always someone that will tell you it can't be done. No matter the goal, no matter the dream. There's no end to those who don't believe that what you aspire to can be accomplished. Your response? Do it anyway.

. . . to live positively we must get beyond the pain of the past and embrace the possibilities of the moment, allowing us to create a future!

Naysayers and failures don't have to be defining.

Most of those naysayers haven't really achieved anything of note themselves. Because they've not experienced success, they doubt that you can. Some just feel so bad about themselves that they can't bear the idea that you might win. But even if they have won themselves, it doesn't mean they know you or your dream well enough to determine that you won't make it. Consider theses notable errors in judgement:

Bishop Wright

He was a prominent figure in the 1800's and in demand as a guest lecturer. He was asked by a major university to address the student body. His topic: "The End of the World."

The premise of Bishop Wright's speech was that surely the end of the world was near due to the fact that all the great inventions that could possibly be invented had already been invented. Since mankind had reached the apex of his intellectual prowess, God was soon to bring the curtain down.

Though a prominent man, Bishop Wright was not beyond questioning. A young student shouted out, "Man has yet to fly!"

Well, the Bishop didn't appreciate that comment. His reply, "If God had wanted man to fly, He would have given him wings!"

Oops. Aren't we glad his sons, Orville and Wilbur, didn't think like their father?

> Consider the headline of the Boston Globe in 1857: "Energy Crisis Looms! World To Go Dark! Whale Blubber Scarce!"

How much would ever really get accomplished if naysayers were listened to? Not much, my friend.

To do great, seemingly impossible things, you've got to have a great belief in yourself and in the value of the goal. What others say doesn't really matter most of the time.

Another thing; don't let failure stop you either. When I was a kid, the greatest baseball hero of the day was Mickey Mantle. Yet failure was a companion to Mantle in his career. Consider that Mickey Mantle struck out 1,710 times, and had 1,734 walks while he played for the New York Yankees. Now, if you figure that he had come to bat 3,444 times and didn't hit the ball and the average player gets about 500 attempts to bat during a season, then the renowned Mickey Mantle played seven years without ever hitting the ball!

Those failures didn't keep Mantle from becoming one of the all-time greats of baseball.

As you attempt things there will always be those telling you it can't be done and sometimes circumstances will confirm their negative assessments; however, you owe it to yourself to stay true to your passion. Naysayers and failures don't have to be defining. If it's a good thing, and doable by your own assessment, do it anyway.

You Deserve It!

You want to get ahead in your job? You want to be noticed as someone with a lot to offer? You want to stand out as a person of value? Well then, do your job as if you owned the company.

There once was a fellow that worked for a window-washing firm. This business would contract with condominium complexes to do windows on a unit-by-unit basis.

One day the crew were washing the windows of a particular unit when the owner of the condominium rushed out and angrily told the window washer, "I didn't order this service. I have no intention of paying you for this work."

The fellow washing the window quickly responded with a brilliant reply, "That's okay. Every time we do a condominium complex, we do one extra unit 'on the house' to show owners such as yourself what a fine job we do, and to show you what you are missing."

Well, you know, that just impressed the socks off the condominium owner of that unit. He immediately signed on as a customer to have his windows washed the next time they came to the complex.

That window washer's employer heard of his action and thought so much of what he had done that they made his idea a part of their regular marketing. The company's business expanded and the window washer earned a raise.

When you want to stand out you must first stand up. You've got to demonstrate your value by working as though you owned the company.

Success gravitates to the people that behave as though they deserved it. Start to look for ways that you can make a contribution and you'll soon see that positive things will happen.

Get the big picture. Your work matters and you can become very successful by having the right attitudes.

Imagine yourself walking up to a construction site. You spot a man shoveling dirt. You ask him,

Success gravitates to the people that behave as though they deserved it.

"What are you doing?" He gives you a "You're pretty stupid" look and says, "Digging a ditch!"

You walk over to another man doing the same thing and ask him, "What are you doing?" His reply is a little less abrasive. "I'm makin' a living. Just makin' a living. Gotta feed the wife and kids, you know."

You spot a third man doing the same thing. "What are you doing?" He, with energy and pride says, "Sir, I am creating part of a masterful set of irrigation channels that are going to turn this dry ol' valley into a garden rich with produce to feed the world's hungry!"

Which of the three fellows digging the ditch do you think will be the most successful? If you owned a company, which one would you hire? See the big picture. Work in such a way as to illustrate your value.

Don't Worry, Be Happy

Several years ago I went to beautiful Rome, the ancient city of artistic splendor. I relished every moment spent along the narrow streets, savoring every turn and twist, inhaling every fragrance and being enthralled by each new sight. Like a child at Christmas, I excitedly anticipated what would come next.

It was all too much to absorb, a sensory overload of creative genius. None greater than the prolific work of Michaelangelo. Overwhelming is the best word to describe his contribution. To stroll the halls of the Vatican and pass through the grandeur of the Sistine Chapel, is to appreciate the imprint and influence of this great artist.

His works are many, his sculptures splendid. David, Day and Night, Madonna of Bruges, Twilight and Dawn, La Pieta, Medici, Madonna and Child. My favorite statue of his is located in the Church of St. Peter and the Chains. The great Moses, a chiseled masterpiece of the man of God coming down from the Mount of Sinai, ready to present to the people of Israel the Law that would guide them.

To look at this work one must take time. Like examining a fine jewel, the light has to be just right and it must be seen from all angles. Truly, you see Moses and that is a veritable feast for the eyes.

As wondrous as it is, Michaelangelo wasn't happy with the result of his efforts. When he had finished, he is reputed to have angrily cried out, "Why doest thou not speak?" He wanted the great Moses to come to life. He felt he had failed and in his anger he took his chisel and struck the knee of the statue! The mark remains as a reminder of his dissatisfaction.

I understand this emotionally fueled attitude. People who are creative and desire to achieve are often dissatisfied with their efforts. They are often harsh and critical of themselves when perfection isn't attained.

Winners in life don't allow their perfectionistic drives to so frustrate them that they quit. Michaelangelo didn't. He continued working until he died. Never allowing his quest for perfection to destroy the art he *could* create. Believe me when I say that Michaelangelo was too hard on himself when it came to his Moses. It does indeed speak to you.

You may have a perfectionistic streak that you've allowed to get in the way of accomplishment. "If it can't be done perfectly, why try?" Don't fall into that trap. Sometimes we're just too close to our work to see the real worth of it. Michaelangelo was.

Enjoy the journey of effort and believe your work matters. Do your best and accept the results.

Can You Fix It?

To succeed in business, you've got to help people solve problems; you've got to meet their needs.

Over the years, I've had many opportunities to sit down, one on one, and help people solve their problems. I've brainstormed with business people on ways to enhance their efforts and refine their marketing strategy. I've seen a lot of people with a lot of needs. I've learned that if you help them, you will benefit in the end.

Some years ago Victor Kiam worked as a salesman for Playtex. He sold girdles and bras throughout the state of Mississippi. One particular day he went into a little shop hoping to make a sale. The owner didn't respond well. What did he do? Well, he grabbed a broom and swept Kiam out the door.

Kiam was a bit perplexed at this reception and began to inquire of other sales reps as to why this man had gotten so upset with him.

It seems Kiam's predecessor had done such a thorough job of selling, that the shop owner was overstocked and unable to move the merchandise. The man was mad because he felt he'd been had. He spent all his time and capital on inventory and resented it. Kiam just happened to be the guy the shop owner decided to take it out on.

Well, Victor Kiam didn't become a master salesman by doing nothing. He contacted one of his larger accounts and convinced them to pur-

Winners in life don't allow their perfectionistic drives to so frustrate them that they quit.

If you want to succeed in business, you must exceed people's expectations.

chase the shop owner's excess inventory. He set this up at no cost to the shop owner. By solving this man's problem, he gained a customer and a friend. His reception the next time he visited was much more pleasant.

If you want to succeed in business, you must exceed people's expectations. Solve their problems; meet their needs. You'll win when you help them to win.

Excuse Me!

Don Meredith, former NFL player and Monday night football commentator once said, "If 'ifs' and 'buts' were candy and nuts, we'd all have a Merry Christmas." Translation: Excuses don't cut it! You can complain all you want to, that "if" you had more money or were taller or could just get the right break, you'd be successful. You can protest, "But you don't understand"; "But I just can't"; "But I don't have. . . "

"Ifs" and "buts" are poor excuses for not winning. Rather than making excuses when you fail, simply accept graciously that things didn't work out and move on. Because I write and speak on success, people often assume that I believe a person will always succeed at every endeavor. Well, I don't believe that. Truthfully, we fail more often than succeed. Sometimes our failures serve to redirect us; they can be very helpful in maturing us and can enable us to do things better the next time.

The question we should ask ourselves when tackling any task is, "Am I doing my best?" In the final analysis, that's the only thing that matters. Excuses are for people who don't do their best and fail. Winners may fail but they don't make excuses, that's why they're winners.

The 1988 Super Bowl matched the Broncos against the Redskins. John Elway played like a man driven by excellence. He didn't quit when things didn't go his way. Despite his best efforts, the game victory was not to be his. After the game, he had good things to say about the Broncos and the Redskins. He didn't make excuses; he didn't lay blame. He and his team had done their best and their best hadn't won the game. Was he a loser then? I don't think so. Why? He gave the game all he had. The more his team fell behind, the harder he fought. That makes him a winner.

Winning is about giving yourself to excellence.

When we make excuses, when we hide behind "ifs" and "buts," we exhibit a lack of character and integrity that left unchecked, will prevent us from living up to our potential. Doing your best is one of the way we heed Shakespeare's words, "To thine own self be true."

You'll have to ***stand-up*** *to* ***stand-out.***

I think we do a disservice to ourselves when we whine instead of win. Winning is about giving yourself to excellence. The words of the poem, "The Person In the Mirror," paint the picture well.

You can't avoid him.
You can't ever get away from him.
Every day you have to report to him.
At the end of your life, he'll be there.
No one else can see him.
No one else matters quite as much.

Meredith had it right, "ifs" and "buts" aren't candy and nuts. If you want to have a Merry Christmas, stop making excuses.

Be SHARP, Stay SHARP

Are you a **SHARP** person? I use the word **SHARP** as an acronym for: **S**uccessful, **H**appy **A**nd **R**eally **P**roductive. Becoming a **SHARP** person requires a *decision;* you must *decide* that you're going to overcome *fear* and refuse to allow circumstances, emotions or the negative opinions of others, to dominate your thoughts about what's possible in your life. You'll have to *stand-up* to *stand-out.* No more hiding behind excuses or wallowing in self-pity. Take charge of your destiny by making the right decisions today.

Becoming a SHARP person is one thing, staying that way is another; Allow me to share ***Stoops' Rules For Staying SHARP:***

1. **Believe**
   The greatest accomplishments are possible only when you believe enough. If you doubt your goals, you'll be sure to falter.
2. **Read**
   Reading opens the mind. Don't make excuses: growing requires effort and reading offers you an unending education. Make it a life-long pursuit.
3. **Network**
   It's not just what you know; it's who you know. Expand your sphere of influence. Make friends by being one. Help everyone you can and they'll help you.

4. **Discipline**
   Learn self-discipline. The world isn't going to be your Mama! Control your time; guard your health; save your money; shut your mouth. Most importantly, open your ears! It takes discipline to listen.
5. **Give**
   Be generous. Refuse to allow greed to govern. It's all right to possess things, it's not all right for things to possess you.
6. **Work**
   Work is a good four letter word. It becomes powerful when done both hard and smart. There is no substitute for honest and honorable effort. Engage your work with morality and sincerity.
7. **Observe**
   Be alert. Opportunities are all around and are often found in the most unlikely of circumstances. They are missed by those who fail to see.
8. **Plan**
   Don't be afraid to ask directions. Plan, set goals, evaluate, plan again. Step-by-step and soon you're walking; nothing but words, you'll only be talking.
9. **Action**
   Do, go, make it so! Don't wait to feel before you take action. Do what needs to be done and let the feelings follow.
10. **Smile**
   Smiling breeds friendliness. Friendly people win. Smiling is an action—step to a better attitude.

These simple rules will enhance your potential for achievement and enable you to be a positive influence in the lives of others.

Are You Too Young or Too Old?

There's no end to the things we allow to stop us. Things that are nothing more than speed bumps or directional signs, we turn into stop signs. One thing that keeps many from trying is age.

Age really is a relative issue. Too young or too old, become the banners people hide under. Consider Pablo Morales. He was considered a rising star in swimming, but at 23 he was washed up. When the 100 meter butterfly event came on television during the 1988 Seoul Olympics, he couldn't even stand to watch.

He had made the U.S. Team in 1984, at the age of 19, and barely missed the gold during the Los Angles games. As the Seoul games awaited him, there was great anticipation on the part of the sports community. He did so poorly in the trials however, he didn't even make the team. His potential seemed spent. A short time later, his mother and greatest supporter, was diagnosed with cancer.

His life seemed to drift for a while when he began to feel again the desire to compete. With only six months to prepare for the 1992 trials for Barcelona, he diligently began to train. When his mother died, he decided to work hard in her honor. At 27 he was old by swimming standards. Yet, with the help of his old swim coach, he worked to win.

With his father holding a picture of his deceased wife, Pablo's mother, Pablo swam furiously the 100 meter butterfly. As he finished, the scoreboard read, "Morales—USA—1." Pablo had the gold. An old man of 27 had achieved his dream.

It's very easy to let things stop you, but just remember, without your consent, things can't win.

Who's Afraid??

Isabel Moore once said, "Life is a one-way street. No matter how many detours you take, none of them leads back. And once you know and accept that, life becomes much simpler." I agree. Life is a progressive experience where the real scenery is straight ahead. What concerns me is those detours. They can become stopping grounds; places where we come to a halt and fail to move on. So many people miss out on the beauty up ahead, because they've been diverted and wound up in an unpleasant place.

One of the most common detours in life is fear. It's a horrible place to spend time; fear has a way of perpetuating itself. In his book, *The Success Journey*, John Maxwell shares this about fear:

> *Fear* breeds *inaction;*
> *Inaction* leads to lack of *experience;*
> Lack of *experience* fosters *ignorance;* and
> *Ignorance* breeds *fear.*

Let's take a few moments to consider this insight about fear. When people take this detour in life, they stop progressing. They choose to stand

Age really is a relative issue.

I believe God has made us to enjoy life to the fullest, and for those that remain jailed by fear, most of the joy is missed.

still and fail to make the necessary decisions that propagate achievement. Fran Tarkenton, former NFL quarterback and current business consultant, says, "Fear causes people to draw back from situations; it brings on mediocrity; it dulls creativity; it sets one up to be a loser in life." Being inactive as a result of fear stops the natural progression of life which is meant to be a forward-moving journey. People who are afraid become inactive and spend most of their time looking backward.

Inactivity forfeits the rich experiences that enable us to grow as individuals. When people are afraid, they won't tackle new projects; they avoid challenges that could stretch them beyond where they are. I see this as tragic because I believe God has made us to enjoy life to the fullest, and for those that remain jailed by fear, most of the joy is missed.

Fear is natural and should be expected, but we are ruined by it when we allow it to detour us from going forward. Dr. Susan Jefferies speaks of the fear that comes from progress when she said, "As long as I continue to push out into the world, as long as I continue to stretch my capabilities, as long as I continue to take risks in making my dreams come true, I am going to experience fear." So, it's natural, but it doesn't have to stop us!

As fear breeds inactivity, inactivity leads to missing out on the rich experiences of life. Missing out on those experiences keeps us ignorant. Ignorance is a dangerous place! Because of fear we don't do what we ought to do and we miss out and fail to learn what we need in order to achieve. Ignorance in turn keeps us afraid. It's a vicious circle.

If you're going to be blessed, you must get back on the straight road of life. Get off the side road of fear. How? Stop worrying about what might be and start dealing with what is. Former UCLA basketball coach John Wooden said, "Do not let what you cannot do interfere with what you can do."

The next suggestion is to boldly embrace what needs to be done and do it now. Mark Twain said, "Do something every day that you don't want to do. This is the golden rule for acquiring the habit of doing your duty without pain."

So, on the one-way street of life, determine to get on with it. Quit looking back and being afraid. Start moving forward even if it's only one step at a time.

Failure Doesn't Have to Be Final

As a boy, I read the classic Dale Carnegie book, *How to Win Friends and Influence People*, which has sold over 15 million copies over the last sixty years. It still remains a "must" read for anyone wanting to improve their people skills. The Dale Carnegie Institute For Effective Speaking and Human Relations trains people all over the world and remains a valuable resource for individuals and companies wishing to enhance their effectiveness.

Dale Carnegie's life provides us with a great story of overcoming failure. During his early life he was plagued with poverty. His dream was to attend teacher's college in Warrensburg, Missouri. He managed to do so but had to live at home to save money. He rode to school each day on horseback and worked hard to make his way through.

He had always been interested in public speaking and entered a number of speech contests, hoping to gain recognition for his achievements. He never won a single contest, but learned something of value each time he failed.

Though he labored long and hard, he failed Latin and wasn't allowed to graduate. He then moved to New York City, hoping to make his mark in acting and sales. Again and again he failed to achieve, but learned something of value from every defeat.

Then one day he applied for a job at the YMCA, teaching public speaking. Because he lacked experience, he wouldn't receive the usual two dollars a session, but if he proved to be effective and the students stayed with the program, he would make money. Again he worked hard, teaching and writing. The booklets he wrote would later become best-selling books. This time he was successful.

Giles Kemp and Edward Cloflin, in their book, *Dale Carnegie: The Man Who Influenced Millions*, wrote, "Carnegie rose to fame as one of the most effective trainers of speakers and one of the best-selling authors of all time. Two keys enabled him to turn failure into success: his unwillingness to be stopped by failure, and his willingness to learn from failure."

I believe those two keys have great potential for transformation for anyone wanting to become winners in life. Failure doesn't have to be final, and for those willing to learn something from the experience, failure can prove to have been a friend.

Eyes Wide Open

We live in an extremely negative world. It's easy to see things from a dark, despairing perspective given that we are by nature pessimistic. A Murphy's Law mentality seems to reign over the land. No place is this more evident than in the news media.

One February some time ago, the Washington Post ran a headline that stated, "US Economy Gains, Adds 40,000 Jobs In One Month: Report Spurs Fears." You'd think that economic growth would be good news, but not so from the Post's perspective. They feared increased job growth would lead to escalating interest rates. When job growth slowed several months later, the New York Times ran a headline that stated the decline was "stirring concern."

When the dollar is weak, the media projects fear that foreign investors will flee. When the dollar is strong, fear that we won't be able to maintain economic stability in the foreign-exchange market prevails. No matter what the news, it all seems to be bad news.

The way we decide to look at things has a profound effect upon our lives. Our world view is tied to our actions. Sometimes negative experiences have a way of shaping the way we look at the world, taking the wind out of our sails. That once happened to Lee Iacoca.

Lee Iacoca had managed to climb the corporate ladder of Ford and was highly esteemed throughout the auto industry. He had been responsible for the development of one of the greatest success stories for Ford: the Mustang.

Things turned on Mr. Iacoca when Ford abruptly fired him. After many years of success, that negative experience almost derailed Iacoca. The Chrysler Company offered him the top job at the struggling Auto Company, but Iacoca just couldn't see it. His world view had been temporarily altered by negativity.

Things looked so bad at Chrysler that Iacoca told his wife, "I don't think anyone could turn this company around." Mrs. Iacoca replied, "I'm sure Mr. Ford will be glad to hear that." That simple statement re-ignited the fire in Lee Ioacca and he took the job. We all know how his efforts paid off!

When everyone around you puts a negative spin on things, be aware that it is optimism that spurs us motivationally to take positive action to achieve. Don't allow anyone or anything to determine your world view in a negative way. Choose to see with hope.

The way we decide to look at things has a profound effect upon our lives.

Are You Paying Attention?

Being a good communicator involves a great deal of skill. Not only must you be able to speak well and write clearly, you must also be able to pay attention. When we fail to employ this crucial skill, all kinds of erroneous messages can be sent.

When everyone around you puts a negative spin on things, be aware that it is optimism that spurs us motivationally to take positive action to achieve.

Consider the following messages that were conveyed because someone failed to pay attention:

> In a Paris hotel elevator: *Please leave your values at the front desk.*
>
> In a Bucharest hotel lobby: *The lift is being fixed for the next day. During that time we regret that you will be unbearable.*
>
> In a hotel in Athens: *Visitors are expected to complain at the office between the hours of 9 and 11 a.m. daily.*
>
> Outside a Hong Kong tailor shop: *Ladies may have a fit upstairs.*
>
> On the menu of a Swiss restaurant: *Our wines leave you nothing to hope for.*

Some of my favorite examples of failure to pay attention can be found in Church bulletins:

> *To those of you who have children and don't know it, we have a nursery downstairs.*
>
> *The Reverend Merriweather spoke briefly, much to the delight of the audience.*
>
> *Remember in prayer the many who are sick of our church community.*
>
> *The ladies of the church have cast off clothing of every kind, and they can be seen in the church basement Friday afternoon.*
>
> *This being Easter Sunday, we will ask Mrs. White to come forward and lay an egg on the altar.*
>
> *Don't let worry kill you off. Let the church help.*

Paying attention is active interest.

Paying attention is active interest. Showing interest in what you're doing is important if you hope to be effective and productive in your interpersonal relationships both at home and at work.

Here are some tips to help in paying attention:

- **Concentrate**—We have the capacity to think four times faster than we speak, so it's not surprising that our minds wander when people are speaking with us. To counter this natural tendency, we must concentrate on what is being said and refuse to be diverted.
- **Focus Your Eyes on the Person Speaking**—This helps you concentrate and allows the person speaking to you to feel they have your attention.
- **Write It Down**—Writing down details to a project enables us to be more exact in carrying out the project. It also serves two important purposes in the business world: 1) It gives people speaking to you immediate gratification because it conveys that you intend to implement what's being said, and 2) it assures that person you won't forget.

Are you paying attention? If not, you may be losing a lot. Careers are derailed, marriages are destroyed and valuable life lessons are delayed, all because attention wasn't being paid. Don't send out the wrong messages and end up with confusion.

Is It Half Full or Half Empty?

Life can be tough and troubles often comprise its content. The resounding lament of "Why me?" can be heard from many a troubled sojourner as they encounter each trial and tribulation along the well-worn path of living. The better question should be, "Why *not* me?" Given the fact that we live in a fallen world where heartache and pain are the common currency, shouldn't we be surprised when we don't suffer?

The pessimist sees the sufferings associated with human life and adopts negativity in the guise of just being a realist. Their "realism" sours their approach to life and lessens the likelihood of their being able to prevail when pain arrives. The right attitude that looks for the joy in the midst of sorrow allows for greater meaning in living and is the more realistic approach, in spite of what the pessimists might say. It's easy to understand the pessimist's pessimism, but how can we become positive, having a more profitable attitude?

Dr. Victor E. Frankl, a man who experienced three years at Auschwitz, as well as other Nazi prison camps, writes of his observations in those sanctuaries of horrors:

> "We who lived in concentration camps can remember the men who walked through the huts comforting others, giving away their last piece of bread. They have been few in number, but they offer sufficient proof that everything can be taken from a man but one thing: the last of the human freedoms—to choose one's attitude in any given set of circumstance, to choose one's own way."

The choice of attitude is our own. Circumstances or the actions of others cannot alter our view of life without our consent.

Success and significance come to those who will accept the responsibility for choosing the right attitude. To give when it seems everyone else is taking; to love when it seems like hate is the way to go. This approach may seem naive to some and foolish to many, but I believe it makes sense and has within it the greater potential for making us better, sparing us from the awful consequence of becoming bitter.

Being a servant, a giver, someone who really cares, opens the doors of opportunity and closes the doors of energy depleting, self-defeating pessimism. Life is too short to be a whiner when we were created to be winners.

So, You Had a Tough Childhood!

Obstacles and hardships are common to us all, some more so than others. This simple observation leads to another; far too many of us are making excuses for the lack of success in the present, based upon the pain of the past.

While it may be true that some have had a particularly difficult life, it isn't true that *that* predetermines failure. On the contrary, difficulties, hardships and major obstacles can become contributors to our success.

Success and significance come to those who will accept the responsibility for choosing the right attitude. To give when it seems everyone else is taking; to love when it seems like hate is the way to go.

Where there is no challenge, no obstacles or hardships, there is but limited growth and development.

Some years ago, a study by Victor and Mildred Goertzel, entitled *Cradles Of Eminence,* explored the childhood experience and home environment of 300 highly successful people. Their names are easily recognizable: Franklin D. Roosevelt, Helen Keller, Winston Churchill, Albert Schweitzer, Gandhi, Einstein and Freud.

These findings are fascinating and deserve to be noted next time we're tempted to focus on our weaknesses or past pain in an attempt to rationalize failure. Consider the following:

- Three-fourths of the children studied had to contend with poverty, overbearing parents, broken homes, or rejection.
- Seventy-four of the eighty-five writers of fiction and drama, as well as sixteen of twenty poets came out of home situations where tension and dysfunction between parents was the norm.
- Over one-fourth had to deal with physical handicaps such as deafness, blindness or crippled limbs.

So you see, obstacles and hardships don't have to lead to failure. William A. Ward was right when he said, "Adversity causes some men to break; others to break records."

Biologists refer to this as "the adversity principle." It seems that in their studies among plants and animals, well-being is not always an advantage to a species. Where there is no challenge, no obstacles or hardships, there is but limited growth and development. One recent survey discovered that 87% of the people questioned said "a painful event (death, illness, break-up, divorce, etc.) caused them to find a more positive meaning in life."

To become all that you can be, you must live in the present and stop making excuses. We will always have problems, but problems exist to be solved. Churchill once remarked, "Kites rise highest against the wind—not with it." Don't be afraid to fly!

Huh? What Did You Say?

Of all our bodily organs, the one requiring the most energy is the inner ear. Why you ask? Perhaps it is because listening is so important. Too few people do it very well and there's nothing worse than being in conversation with someone that listens in a superficial manner.

It was just such a problem that once prompted President Franklin Roosevelt to play a prank on guests filing through a White House reception line. The President decided that people weren't actually paying attention to him when he greeted them, so as he shook hands with each guest, he gave them a big smile and said, "I murdered my grandmother this morning." No one noticed! They gave the standard responses such as "How lovely!" or "Keep up the good work." Roosevelt got a big laugh out of it but I doubt those who blundered in their listening skills were very proud.

Researchers indicate that people listen best when they perceive the topic to be of *value* or *unusual* or *threatening.* Achievers learn to regard every encounter as having merit and they listen attentively to gain understanding.

One example of a good listener was the late Ray Kroc, founder of McDonald's. Kroc was always looking for a product that would uniquely meet the needs of a vast marketplace. Sometimes he was successful, sometimes not so successful. During the 1950's, he decided that McDonald's needed to offer a dessert, and what would be better than his own mom's Kolacky, a Bohemian delicacy she made for him. One problem, no one bought it!

Another Kroc innovation was the Hulaburger; two slices of cheese and a grilled pineapple ring on a toasted bun! Never heard of it? No wonder, no one bought it! Another failure.

The menu McDonald's has come to be famous for, the Big Mac, Egg McMuffin and other favorites came about not as result of Ray Kroc's ingenuity, but by *listening* to the franchise holders out in the trenches of the marketplace. Listening allowed Kroc to stumble into the great wealth builder that McDonald's has proved to be.

Listening has great value in enhancing your likelihood of achievement. Besides, as Wilson Mizner once said, "A good listener is not only popular everywhere, but after a while he knows something."

Ignition of the Soul

Enthusiasm is the purposeful fuel of achievement. By being enthused, we progress toward the goals of our life with a will to win. It is enthusiasm that drives the ordinary to do the extraordinary. It is prized by all as a crucial ingredient to success. Vince Lombardi, famed coach of the Green Bay Packers, expressed the place he held enthusiasm when he said, "If you aren't fired with enthusiasm, you will be fired with enthusiasm."

Achievers learn to regard every encounter as having merit, and they listen attentively to gain understanding.

When we engage in tasks, we must decide to be enthusiastic about our endeavor. How will we persist if we lack the key dynamic that makes for victory?

So what is enthusiasm? It can best be described as the ignition of the soul. It is a world view; it is a decision. It sees life as full of possibilities and embraces opportunities with gusto. It drives the possessor when all circumstances stand in the way. It is often the determining force in a confrontation with challenge.

The conductor, Eugene Ormandy, was once directing the Philadelphia Orchestra when in a moment of great passion he dislocated his shoulder. That's enthusiasm!

When we engage in tasks, we must decide to be enthusiastic about our endeavor. How will we persist if we lack the key dynamic that makes for victory?

Too often, we fail because we approach common deeds as though the outcome of our efforts is of no matter. This is often the very cause of our mediocrity. We need to realize that our enthusiastic approach to a problem is half the solution.

I like the words of Ralph Waldo Emerson when he wrote:

> "Enthusiasm is one of the most powerful engines of success. When you do a thing, do it with your might. Put your whole soul into it. Stamp it with your own personality. Be active, be energetic, be enthusiastic and faithful, and you will accomplish your objective. Nothing great was ever achieved without enthusiasm"

To be enthusiastic you have to go deep into your desire. How bad do you want a thing? How passionate are you about your goal? Do you feel so strongly that you might explode? Excited? Thrilled to win? Pulling the emotion from way down in your toes? These questions direct us to the heart of enthusiasm.

Jerry Zaks, a Tony Award-winning director, relates an experience he had during his first acting role. He had a small role in Fiddler on the Roof. He was a part of the tour that starred Zero Mostel. He said, "I had one critical line, 'Even a poor tailor is entitled to some happiness.' I was supposed to shout it at Zero, right in his face, and I was sure I was giving my all. But every night, just before the line, he'd whisper, 'Give it to me. Come on, give it to me.'

"Finally I got so angry I just lost it. I stood up on my toes. I went white; I screamed; I was actually spitting in that face I detested so much, 'Even a poor tailor is entitled to some happiness!' And this time, the audience roared, and Zero said to me under his breath, 'Thaaat's it! Thaaat's it!"

You see, enthusiasm comes from passion. Tap into your passion. Achievement is the result of those who've learned this important lesson.

Sometimes You Gotta Laugh

There sure are a lot of things to be stressed-out about. Pressures in the workplace, in the home and even in areas that are supposed to be leisure experiences. Sometimes all the pressure can seem overwhelming. What can you do about it? Well, try laughing more!

Many people remember Dan Jansen, 1994 Winter Olympic gold medalist. He wanted to succeed in his quest for achievement, so he did the things that are normally associated with excelling sports performance. But sometimes doing what normally works isn't enough. For Jansen, that meant consulting sports psychologist, James Loehr.

Armed with the knowledge that humor relaxes and relieves stress, Dr. Loehr recommended that Jansen loosen-up and laugh more.

Research from the University of Colorado reveals that when we laugh, our brain releases chemicals that have pain-reduction benefits. Laughter also promotes healing. During periods of intense stress and fearfulness, another chemical works to block the healing chemicals, and thus, we become more prone to long-term illness.

Dr. Norman Cousins, an editor many years ago for the noted Saturday Review, was struck with a disease that doctors had no cure for. It was the early 1960's, and it seemed that a sentence of death had been given to him. Dr. Cousins however, understood the effects of negative emotions on the human body and reasoned that positive emotions could have a healing quality. He set out on a grand experiment that consisted of watching hours of Marx Brother movies and "Candid Camera" reruns.

He learned about his disease and he learned to laugh. He wrote about his experiences in his book, *Anatomy of an Illness as Perceived by the Patient.* One of the things he discovered that benefited him was that a ten minute belly laugh could give him two hours of painless sleep. No small gain for someone in pain!

Another interesting finding that's recently been discovered is that children laugh an average of 400 times a day, whereas adults laugh only 15 times a day! Apparently, life knocks the fun out of us as we grow older.

We must lighten up and look at life with humor. It takes a willful choice. Some will find it easier than others, but all of us can do it.

The bright side of life, the essence of humor in every situation, has the ability to take the string out of stressful experiences. So, we need to laugh more.

We take life so seriously because of the circumstances and events that come into our path; our feelings are errant guides to surviving those hard moments. We must lighten up and look at life with humor. It takes a willful choice. Some will find it easier than others, but all of us can do it.

I remember so well the day President Ronald Reagan was shot by a would-be assassin. I was holding a funeral in a small town in east-central Indiana. The television happened to be on in the funeral director's office and there, replayed for our eyes, was the tragic event. What stood out most to me, as I later digested the many details of the shooting, was the President's humorous attitude as he was being wheeled into the emergency room, and then on into surgery. It is reported that the President looked up at the doctors that were scurrying to give him care, and said, "I hope all of you are Republicans!" While I don't discount the skillful medical expertise of the doctors attending to Mr. Reagan, I can't help but believe that it was his attitude that had the decisive role in his recovery.

When you're stressed-out and feeling overwhelmed, try laughing out loud. It won't make your problems go away, you'll just be able to weather them better. Refuse the rule of circumstances and embrace the lighter side. Hugh Downs made the point well when he said, "*A happy person is not a person in a certain set of circumstances, but rather a person with a certain set of attitudes.*"

The Shoe Shine Sizzle

As a boy, I shined shoes at an old barber shop on the east side of Indianapolis. The barber shop was truly one of those rustic, "Floyd the Barber" kind of shops. It was heated by a pot-bellied stove, stoked with wood and coal. At the end of the day, the boys and I would sweep up the hair from the day's business, and throw it into the fire. It wasn't a pleasant aroma.

It was in that barber shop, I first learned the rudiments of good salesmanship. There were several of us shoe shine boys vying for the business. In those days, more men wore dress shoes than they do now and it wasn't too difficult to convince them of the need to keep those shoes shining. At a quarter a shine, it was a bona-fide bargain.

On a good day, I could get about two, maybe three dollars. The adventure wasn't getting the opportunity to shine a fellow's shoes. It was in doing such a good job that you could make the customer feel special, like he had just received the best shine possible anywhere. The tip was the goal. Getting the approval for a job well done would be shown by the giving of a tip.

How to go about it? Well, to shine a pair of shoes isn't a complicated thing. After getting the job, you proceed to wash the shoes off. You firmly but gently rub the appropriate polish deep into the leather, massaging the shoes so as to make them eager for the shine. Then you begin to brush the polish in. This will ensure a deep, rich gloss. You would also apply a liquid polish to the rim of the soles. All very straightforward.

The real secret to a great shine and the earning of a tip was in the dance of the shoe shine rag. If you could make the rag dance in a way that spoke of a true event, not just a regular shine—but an event, something to be remembered, then not only would the customer be pleased with the shine, but more importantly, he would be entertained.

A good steak house sells the sizzle. So does a good shoe shine boy, or for that matter, any good salesperson.

Make no mistake, everybody wants a good product; but people want to be entertained as well. Entertainment is about an engagement of the mind. It's about capturing the attention of another, so that for a brief moment, they're distracted from their usual concerns and delighted by what they're experiencing.

The Shoe Shine Sizzle is about selling. Giving people a good product with good service in such a way that they'll have a good time in the process. There's no law that says that free enterprise has to be dull, nor should it be unethical. If you make what you do interesting and honest, you'll enjoy the journey.

Make no mistake, everybody wants a good product; but people want to be entertained as well.

Chapter Four 4

Perseverance

Don't Stop Trying

Growing up, my mother always made an effort to take me places. She would take me to wrestling matches (I was a real fan), to movies, to old Willard Park to swim, and to free concerts. I remember one special time when we went to hear Porter Wagoner at the outdoor theater at Garfield Park, on the south side of Indianapolis.

I grew up with country music because my mother was a fan. She loved the Grand Ole Opry and Midwestern Hayride, and her favorite singers were people like Ernest Tubb, Little Jimmy Dickens and Hank Williams. Well, Porter Wagoner was one of her favorites also. So, off we went to the concert.

At that time, Porter Wagoner had a television show and he had a new girl singer that became a star. Her name was Dolly Parton. She was one of nineteen children from the hills of Tennessee. She did the commercial announcements for the show. She pitched the laundry detergent, Breeze. The unique thing about Breeze was that with every box, you got a free towel and washcloth. My mother thought that was a fine deal. My mother loved Porter, but for obvious reasons, I loved Dolly!

That girl from Tennessee has come a long way since those days on the Porter Wagoner show. She has overcome many obstacles and gone on to build a million dollar kingdom with the creation of Dollywood. Her records have sold millions of copies, her concerts have always been sold out and she even became successful in the movies.

Once, while doing a television special, she was asked by a fan, why she had become successful when so many other poor mountain folk had not. Her answer is classic. "I never stopped trying," she said. "And I never tried stopping."

I like people who refuse to quit. They inspire me. It's so easy to whine about how difficult things are in our lives. It's common to give a long list of "why" we can't succeed and excuse our lack of incentive because for us, life's just been too tough.

Well, I've got encouraging words for you the next time you find yourself whining about how difficult things are for you: Get over it!

Life is too short to miss out on blessings because we've become neck-deep in a pool of self-pity. Dolly is a great example and those words of hers are profound. If you stop trying you'll never win anything. If you try stopping you'll come up short every time.

Life is too short to miss out on blessings because we've become neck-deep in a pool of self-pity.

Winners aren't whiners. They expect to be blessed. They even get excited about laundry detergent because there might be a free gift in the box.

Never Quit

"The basic rules for success may be defined as follows: Know what you want. Find out what it takes to get it. Act on it. And persevere."

Francois Pasqualini

Perseverance is one of the most underrated qualities of a winner in the minds of many. When you listen to most folk pontificating about what it takes to be successful, you'll hear things like, brains, talent, contacts or lucky breaks. Few will mention perseverance. But the truth is, all the brains, talent, contacts and lucky breaks won't matter much, if you quit too soon.

The 1998 NBA championships illustrate the place of perseverance in winning. I just want to go on record as a staunch Indiana Pacers fan. I wanted them to win with all my heart. It didn't happen. What did happen however, was fascinating to watch.

Michael Jordan of the Chicago Bulls is, without doubt, one of the greatest athletes of all time. The Utah Jazz played hard but it would be Jordan and the Bulls that would come away with the championship. Their sixth NBA trophy!

Though Jordan is skilled to a level not many can come close to, it is his perseverance, fueled by a competitive desire to win, that has determined his place in world-class basketball. It was amazing to watch the artistry of the tonguewagging virtuoso pushing himself to win in spite of exhaustion and fierce competition.

Jordan is remarkable in his perseverance partly because he has known defeat; he's tasted failure and he's not allowed it to stop him. He knows through experience that sometimes all you need to do to win is not quit until the game is over.

Thomas Edison had that same persevering spirit. Once, after much failure in a series of experiments, Edison remarked to a coworker, "We haven't failed yet. We now know one thousand things that won't work, so we're that much closer to finding what will." I can see better at night because of Edison's light, because he wouldn't quit!

But the truth is, all the brains, talent, contacts and lucky breaks won't matter much, if you quit too soon.

If you lack perseverance, let me suggest some things to develop:

1. Find your purpose. Discover why you're here and what you do best.
2. Become feverishly passionate about your purpose. Let the desire for your purpose fill you up.
3. Lay out in a detailed plan *how* you're going to fulfill your purpose. What are the action-steps you'll take today?
4. Filter all the negative, discouraging pollutants that would stand in your way of achieving your purpose.
5. Surround yourselves with honest but affirming people. People who will help you to fan into flame the purpose for which you've been made.

These simple suggestions will help you develop the perseverance you need to become the achiever you were meant to be.

Too Old? Nah!

On my desk in my office I have a rock. Inscribed upon it are the words, "Never, Never Quit." I keep it there to remind me of one of the most important principles of success. Failures don't a failure make; quitting a failure makes.

In the 1880's, a Polish engineer by the name of Ernest Malinowski, was consulted along with many other engineers, to give opinions about the possibility of building a railroad through the formidable Andes Mountains. All of the engineers, with the exception of Malinowski, said the project couldn't be done.

Ernest Malinowski was an engineer who enjoyed a great reputation. He was at the time sixty years old and the representatives of the participating nations were concerned that he was too old for such an enormous undertaking. Malinowski, however, convinced them otherwise.

When Malinowski turned seventy, construction began. This massive enterprise required sixty-two tunnels, and thirty bridges. Just one of the tunnels measured 4,000 feet in length and was 15,000 feet above sea level!

Construction had to be halted twice because of revolutions and Malinowski, at one point, had to flee for his life. But nothing was going to stop this grand endeavor. In spite of many obstacles, the railroad is considered one of the greatest engineering accomplishments in the world. Malinowski refused to quit and victory followed.

All of us face challenges that are fraught with obstacles; and the struggle to achieve a worthwhile goal is often daunting; nevertheless, we must refuse the temptation to quit.

Over the years of my life, I've set numerous goals and I've had the pleasure of accomplishing many of them. I've set many new ones for the future and I can tell you that none of them are small, nor will they be easy. But I've learned that while I may not reach every goal, I'll probably reach most of them just because of a resolute refusal to quit.

I challenge you, as we enter another year, to aim for the meaningful things you've always wanted to achieve and be adamant enough to rule out quitting and I think you'll discover, as I have, that you win the day more often than not. May God bless you for a successful year ahead.

You've Gotta Have Heart!

"Aerodynamics have proven that the bumblebee cannot fly. The body is too heavy and the wings are too weak. But the bumblebee doesn't know that, and it goes right on flying, miraculously."

So says the woman who wears a diamond lapel pin shaped like a bumblebee. She should know, she herself is a miracle of sorts.

She raised three children alone after her first husband walked out on her; later she would remarry twice, but both husbands died, leaving her alone once again. Determined at first to provide for her children, she discovered a giftedness for sales.

Her career began with the prospect of obtaining a free set of children's books. If she sold ten sets she could earn one set. She called upon friends and sold ten sets in two days. She said, "I didn't have books to show them—all I had was my enthusiasm." Over the next nine months she sold $25,000 worth of books, and this occurred during the Great Depression of the 1930's!

She went on to succeed at sales with Stanley Home Products and the World Gift Company before she finally launched her own business, Mary Kay Cosmetics, a $950-million-dollar-a-year economic giant. Mary Kay has truly been an em-

All of us face challenges that are fraught with obstacles; and the struggle to achieve a worthwhile goal is often daunting; nevertheless, we must refuse the temptation to quit.

powering force for thousands of women, who have for one reason or another, had a desire to establish their own business.

. . . I just get excited about people who overcome great obstacles to achieve; I do believe Mary Kay personifies the simple sweet ingredient that fuels life; you've got to have heart!

Mary Kay embarked on her great enterprise with noble intentions, "I wasn't interested in the dollars-and-cents part of business—my interest in 1963 was in offering women opportunities that didn't exist anywhere else," she said. Her "interest" has been realized. Mary Kay Cosmetics has made more women millionaires than any other corporation in America!

I've studied entrepreneurs and American success stories for many years and Mary Kay is one of the most inspiring. Perhaps this is because I was raised by a single mother and have seen first hand the struggles that a woman alone goes through trying to make a living; maybe I just get excited about people who overcome great obstacles to achieve; I do believe Mary Kay personifies the simple sweet ingredient that fuels life; you've got to have heart!

The Mary Kay Cosmetic Company has been a blessing to so many because its founder has heart. "I can't believe that God intended for a woman's work to receive only fifty cents on the dollar," she's fond of saying. Her business sense and integrity and passion for people made her company a shining example of motivation and management. The principles that have served to guide her company are outlined in her extraordinary book, *Mary Kay On People Management,* and are profound in their simplicity and illustrate the good heart that is Mary Kay.

- **Recognize the Value of People**
  People are your company's number one asset. When you treat them as you would like to be treated yourself, everyone benefits.
- **Praise Your People to Success**
  Recognition is the most powerful of all motivators. Even criticism can build confidence when it's "sandwiched" between layers of praise.
- **Tear Down That Ivory Tower**
  Keep all doors open. Be accessible to everyone. Remember that every good manager is also a good listener.
- **Be a Risk-Taker**
  Don't be afraid. Encourage your people to take risks, too and allow room for error.

- **Be Sales Oriented**
  Nothing happens in business until somebody sells something. Be especially sensitive to your customers' needs and desires.
- **Be a Problem Solver**
  An effective manager knows how to recognize real problems and how to take action to solve them.
- **Create a Stress-Free Workplace**
  By eliminating stress factors—fear of the boss, unreasonable deadlines, and others—you can increase and inspire productivity.
- **Develop and Promote People from Within**
  Upward mobility for employees in your company builds loyalty. People give you their best when they know they'll be rewarded.
- **Keep Business in Its Proper Place.**
  At Mary Kay Cosmetics the order of priorities is faith, family, and career. The real key to success is creating an environment where people are encouraged to balance the many aspects of their lives.

To grow a business is tough, but learning from the example of one who has done so much in spite of difficulty, can enhance any sincere effort.

The next time you're tempted to throw in the towel and give up because life is hard, just remember that as Mary Kay, and bumblebees, you too can fly!

Down but Not Out

Don't let adversity stop you. Don't give up because things become difficult. It's surprising what stops people. Sometimes it's the most trivial of circumstances; a little adversity and many will run away from a task. Like the woman who was encouraged to join an aerobics class. Her friend had invited her and she responded negatively. "No way," she said. "I tried that once." "What happened?" her friend asked. "I went, and I twisted, hopped, jumped, stretched and pulled," the woman replied. "And by the time I got those darn leotards on, the class was over!"

It's the small stuff that stops most. Interestingly though, is a study that was done some years ago by UCLA. That study found that every great person has had to face some great difficulty or failure in their lives before they became great. Consider the following:

- John Milton went blind before he wrote the classic, *Paradise Lost.*
- Harry Truman had been rejected by West Point, and had failed repeatedly at business, before becoming President of the United States.
- Thomas Edison had a teacher who told his mother that he was "too dumb to learn."
- Mark Twain lived in poverty before becoming a great novelist and humorist.
- Franklin Roosevelt overcame polio to become a great leader.
- Louis Pasteur discovered pasteurization after suffering a paralytic stroke.
- Admiral Byrd endured great loneliness to become a great explorer.
- George Frederick Handel wrote the beautiful "Messiah" while broke and facing debtor's prison, and while paralyzed.

Adversity doesn't have to stop you if you have the right attitude and refuse to quit. Greatness isn't determined merely by how well we do while standing; it is seen in our determination to get back up after being knocked down.

If you want to overcome, you can. I've always enjoyed the music of the British group, the Moody Blues. Justin Hayward, lead singer for the group imparts wisdom when he writes, "Just what you want to be, you will be in the end." If you think you can't, you're right. Don't think that way.

You'll always find someone that's better off than you, and you'll also find many that are worse off. Instead of looking around at others, try looking straight ahead, beyond the momentary adversity. Develop the long view. It's easier to keep going when you do that.

Greatness isn't determined merely by how well we do while standing; it is seen in our determination to get back up after being knocked down.

Chapter Five

Rejection

Keep Going

If you're going to go places; if you're going to make positive strides, you've got to prepare yourself for the inevitable: Rejection. Yeah, you read it right. Rejection. When you push the envelope and dare to be bold in dreaming of a better life, you're going to be rejected. It's a part of the growing process and you'll be better for having experienced it.

Now don't get all worked up thinking I'm just sugar-coating things. There's no magic in being rejected, the benefit comes in the manner you respond to rejection. Achievement comes when you refuse to allow rejection to stop you; when you resolutely go forward even though others are discouraging you.

I've always enjoyed the poetry of Robert Frost, but in 1902, the then 28-year-old writer received a rejection letter from the poetry editor of The Atlantic Monthly. The rejection note read, "Our magazine has no room for your vigorous verse." Of course, that didn't stop Robert Frost.

Consider a fellow by the name of Einstein. In 1905, the University of Bern turned down his Ph.D. dissertation, saying it was fanciful and irrelevant. Of course, that didn't stop Einstein.

Then there was this sixteen-year-old boy in 1894, receiving a stinging note on a report card from his rhetoric teacher at Harrow, in England. It read, "A conspicuous lack of success." Of course, that didn't stop Winston Churchill.

The posture of the winner is that rejection fuels his/her drive. Achievers march to the beat of a different drummer anyway. They don't fall into the parade line of the crowd; they aren't "stopped" by people saying it can't be done.

Achievers seem to possess hope and faith as the sustaining force that keeps them going in spite of rejection. They have the ability to keep going when everyone and everything around them is saying "Give Up!" Though they have discouraging thoughts, they forge ahead.

At the age of 32, standing on the icy shores of Lake Michigan, R. Buckminster Fuller thought of ending his life. He had been expelled from college, and his repeated attempts at business had failed. Standing there, rejected, the thought came to him, "You have no right to eliminate yourself. You do not belong to you."

Achievement comes when you refuse to allow rejection to stop you, when you resolutely go forward even though others are discouraging you.

It was from that low point that Fuller began to climb out of his past. Over the remaining years of his life he had numerous careers: inventor, engineer, mathematician, architect, poet and cosmologist.

That fellow that had been expelled from college won dozens of honorary degrees and was nominated for a Nobel Prize. He wrote two dozen books, traveled around the world 57 times and lectured to millions.

So, if you're going to go places, if you're going to make positive strides, you will be rejected. But don't let that stop you!

Chapter Six

6

Creativity

Row, Row, Row Your Boat

Change comes when pain speaks. What do I mean? Well, each of us resist change and view it as unpleasant. We only submit to it when it becomes too painful to continue along the same route. So, when something becomes uncomfortable or unpleasant, we become open to change. When it becomes unbearable, we embrace change. Achievers however, find ways to initiate change by thinking creatively. They see opportunity when things become different; they respond to hardship by turning on the engine of the mind to discover ways of innovation that improves or transforms an old way of doing something.

Around the turn of the century, a young man named Clarence was smitten by a lovely young woman. He wanted to impress her so he asked her on a picnic.

She was a true beauty. The day they went out she wore a beautiful long dress with about a dozen petticoats. She also was fragrant with the aroma of jasmine and carried a parasol to match her dress. Clarence was beside himself with adoration for this young, gorgeous woman.

He chose a nice location with a lake. There was an island in the middle of the lake, so he secured a row boat and off they went. She, dressed in her finery and he wearing a suit and tie with a high collar.

It was hot and he was sweating as he diligently rowed the boat. She, shaded by her parasol, smiled such a lovely smile that the struggle to row in the heat seemed a small price to pay.

He finally reached the island, jumping out to pull the boat to the shore. He was careful to help her out so as not to get wet, then he turned his attention to setting up all the food and blankets under a beautiful tree. He wanted the day to be just right.

She spoke sweetly, tenderly to him. He relished the sound of her voice. Like well-played music, her words enraptured him and made the moments together seem like paradise.

After finishing their meal she sweetly whispered, "Honey, you forgot the ice cream." "Ice cream," Clarence thought. They were going to enjoy ice cream for dessert.

Love has a way of making us work. Clarence got back into the boat and rowed the long way back across the lake. Drenched in sweat and anxious to get back to his beloved, he looked for a grocery store to buy the ice cream. Having succeeded, he again made the long voyage back to the island. He got out of the boat and climbed the hill, to the shade tree where she sat. She looked at the ice cream and then looked at him. With eyelashes all a flutter she sweetly said, "Honey,

When we're faced with the uncomfortable or the unbearable, we need to think.

you forgot the chocolate syrup." Oh yeah, chocolate syrup!

Love is truly powerful. Off Clarence went. Back into the boat, rowing back across the lake, back to the grocery store, buying the chocolate syrup.

He got back into the boat and began again to row. The sun was beating down upon him as sweat poured from every pore of his body. Blisters on his hands and exhaustion overtaking him, he got to the middle of the lake and suddenly stopped rowing. He just sat there thinking.

Achievers do a lot of thinking. He began to think to himself, "There's got to be a better way." He sat there all afternoon, leaving his sweetie stranded on the island.

At the end of the afternoon he had discovered what needed to be done. He had created mentally what would change boating forever. He invented the outboard motor. Clarence Evinrude would achieve wealth and never have to row another boat unless he wanted to.

Oh, and by the way, he later married the beautiful girl he had stranded.

When we're faced with the uncomfortable or the unbearable, we need to think. We need to tap the creativity that all of us possess and seek to embrace change rather than run from it. Next time you have trouble, see it as an opportunity.

Snakes, Strings and Things

Are you an original thinker? Do you see a problem and ponder about its solution? When faced with an obstacle, do you envision how you can go forward and succeed anyway?

Sadly, most people allow difficulties to stop them from achieving. They just don't see how they might overcome when faced with trouble. It doesn't have to be that way.

Each of us possesses creative abilities that are often untapped and lay dormant within. We must learn to access our creative abilities, and then, we'll be able to solve what at first seemed unsolvable.

Consider for a moment the case of George Ballas. An ordinary fellow who achieved extraordinary results. One day George was getting his car washed. He positioned his vehicle in the line for the automated brushes and sprays to do their work. As his car entered the wash, he settled back in his seat and thought about the things he had to accomplish at home. One of the chores was the trimming and edging of his lawn. This was a particularly hard task because his house was near a bayou, and he had to get down on his hands and knees to trim around the rocks. Difficult and dangerous because a copperhead snake might be hiding there.

As the car wash did its work, Ballas watched the strings of the brushes surround the car. Suddenly, the solution to his problem came to him. "I'd been trying to think of some way to trim the grass around my trees and patio stones on my lawn, and suddenly it came to me. I noticed how the strings in the car wash straightened out when revolving at high speed, yet . . . were flexible enough to reach into every nook and cranny." So, this is how the Weedeater was born!

When Ballas returned home, he took a popcorn can and punched holes in it. He then threaded cord through the holes. Taking the blade off his edger, he bolted the can in place. It tore up the grass and its sound was deafening, but it worked.

Eventually, Ballas decided to market his invention. Twenty distributors turned him down in laughter that anyone would be crazy enough to try cutting grass with nylon string.

In 1971, Ballas invested his own money in the first thirty-pound Weedeater. His son filmed a homemade commercial and Ballas bought twelve thousand dollars worth of airtime on a local T.V. station. Orders poured in. Today, Weedeater, Inc., is a multi-million dollar international corporation.

It all started with a problem that was pondered in a car wash. He had a problem, but every problem has a solution. Ballas tapped into his creative reservoir and the rest is history.

Problems are to be solved. Next time you're faced with a difficulty, get away to a solitary place and begin to think. Relax and think. You'll be surprised what can come to you in the most unlikely places, in the most unlikely way.

We must learn to access our creative abilities, and then, we'll be able to solve what at first seemed unsolvable.

Chapter Seven

Relationships

Being Connected

Being successful is about *being*; not existing but *being*. *Being* is about connectedness. Connection with God, family, friends and receptive to people in general. When all is said and done in life, it's the relationships we had that gave richness to our *being*.

Loneliness in our culture is growing and though people accumulate many trinkets and trophies, they still miss out on the joy of successful *being*.

Real achievement requires a fabric of relationships that bring meaningful content to our time on this planet. Even when we do things poorly, our relationships, if good, determine the degree of enjoyment and satisfaction that we gain.

Consider Roseto, Pennsylvania. Several years ago this small town aroused the curiosity of the scientific community. Why? Well, they had a very low rate of death from coronary heart disease. This fact led the epidemiologists to descend upon Roseto, to study the factors that were contributing to their beating the odds. They expected to find low risk factors for heart disease, instead they found that the Rosetans had terrible health habits.

According to Dr. Joan Borysenko, in her book *Minding the Body, Mending the Mind*, it was the social network of the community that produced the positive results. In Roseto, the extended family was alive and well. People knew one another, talked to one another, listened to one another. If someone needed help, there was no shortage of people to lend a hand. Interestingly, when people moved away from Roseto, their rate of heart attacks rose to predicted levels. The connectedness was more important than their health habits in predicting heart disease.

It would seem that the establishing of meaningful, intimate relationships is at the heart of what it means to be successful. It is foolish to think we can have a rich life without investing in others.

Observation reveals that women are better at *being* than men. They seem to gravitate toward connectedness. Women often develop very elaborate support systems that provide them with many benefits. It's not surprising that women live longer than men.

Married men live longer than single men. Even though men in general don't form relationships easily, a married man has his wife.

I recently enjoyed an article that originally appeared in Redbook and was reprinted in Reader's Digest. Joel Achenback wrote in "*What*

Real achievement requires a fabric of relationships that bring meaningful content to our time on this planet.

Men Secretly Love About Marriage," a list of things men appreciate about their marriages. He noted that women bring *standards* to the house. Men often don't distinguish between a napkin or a paper towel. Their wives bring the discernment. Women bring *comfort.* A macho man still has need of someone to cling to when afraid. Women bring *freedom from freedom.* One of the reasons single men don't live as long as married men is an inability to handle unlimited freedom. Achenback's main point is that women help men to become aware of other *lifeforms.* That is, marriage helps the man move away from self-centeredness to a loving "otherness."

No matter the gender, connectedness is a key to success. One can "be" when there is a purposeful reason to be. When the time for your sojourn on this earth comes to an end, you won't have any regrets about not working more, or possessing more, but many will have more than a little regret at not having loved more.

Make Friends

"In America, the moon is bigger, the sky is higher, the ocean wider." That's what Mrs. Shih always told her two children, Marty and Helen. A few months spent at the American School in Beijing was all she needed to passionately desire to live and prosper in America.

Having already achieved much as an opera star in China, Mrs. Shih knew success. After World War II, she married a Chinese bureaucrat. In 1949, while on government business, she and her husband went to Taiwan and decided to never return to their homeland, which had fallen under the control of the Communists. With only the clothes on their backs, they started over. Her dream was that her children might journey to the United States, and experience the American dream.

Marty and Helen ended up in Los Angeles. Helen had already been there several years attending graduate school. When Marty arrived in 1979, he took $500 his mother gave him for graduate school and with his sister Helen, he invested in a flower stand. The first day in the streets he and his sister sold a small bunch of flowers for $1.99. Not a great beginning. But rather than surrender to a defeatist attitude, he said to himself, "Marty, you will become the McDonald's of the flower industry."

Marty and Helen realized that if they were to be successful they would have to work at building relationships with their customers, one customer at a time. They scoured the phone books, creating a database of everyone with a Chinese name; they asked each customer their name, address, phone number and occasion for their purchase of flowers. When dates of anniversaries or birthdays rolled around, they contacted their customers and reminded them of their special dates and the appropriateness of flowers for the occasion. Of their strategy, Helen said, "We found our reminders were very important to our customers. They appreciated being reminded to send flowers on special occasions to people they loved."

Business, as well as life, is best conducted with a willingness to do everything with excellence and a commitment to serve.

The years have blessed Marty and Helen Shih. They have created many different businesses and in 1997, they hope to move as much as $500 million dollars in products. They built their business on McDonald's model of innovation of product and quick delivery. They've created a vital link to the 9.4 million Asian-American market. Today, they enjoy millionaire status but more importantly, their mother's hope of her children experiencing the American Dream has come true.

The best part of their story is not that they've achieved earthly riches and preside over a formidable business empire; the joy of the story is the journey. They overcame great obstacles to win and they didn't do it on the backs of others. They ascended because they were willing to work hard and risk; they were willing to make mistakes and not excuses; they were willing to serve people, bringing humanity to business. About their success, Marty said, "I would say always having the passion, the dream, the enthusiasm, and not being afraid to make mistakes." He went on to say, "I make hundreds of mistakes. In the early days, I lost half a million dollars making the wrong business decisions. In our companies, workers don't see me as a big business person or as a hero. They see that I make mistakes. I say to them, 'You have to forgive other people for their mistakes, just as you forgive me. We have to keep the servant heart.'"

Business, as well as life, is best conducted with a willingness to do everything with excellence and a commitment to serve. No matter what, you can do your best and shine like a star if you have the desire.

Imagine That!

The most recent research has revealed that our brains have no real memory centers. Instead, memories are distributed throughout our brains. In order to improve your memory, you must learn to associate items in ways that may seem strange but nevertheless, work. For

Our minds are fascinating and most of us never tap into our full potential.

instance, if you wanted to recall a name like "Henshaw," you might picture in your mind a hen wrapped in a shawl. This image will form the memory enabling you to recall the name.

This is not a new system. It was developed by the Greeks to aid in winning oration contests during which they would often be required to speak for several hours without the benefit of notes.

By using this system, you can become more effective in life. People appreciate someone who remembers their name; it also allows for greater business success in that people with sharper memory skills are more likely to get it right the first time.

Another way to develop your brain power is through visualization. No, I'm not talking about going up to a mountain somewhere and contemplating your naval. Rather, I'm referring to seeing in your mind the desired goal you want to achieve; visualizing each part of the desired outcome, incorporating a multi-sensory image—taste, smell and touch. Your mind is especially open to such methods when you first wake up in the morning, or just before you go to sleep.

An illustration of this method can be gleaned from the experience of Major James Nesmith. Major Nesmith had a 90-average golf game but managed to knock 20 strokes off that average. How did he do it? Well, he was captured by the Vietcong and confined for seven long years in a small cell in one of their prison camps.

To keep from going mad, he played 18 holes of golf every day in his mind. He carefully visualized every detail, spending three or four hours on his game. Day after day he played this enjoyable trick on his brain. It would seem that his brain didn't differentiate between whether he was really playing golf or just visualizing it! After getting out of the prison camp, he went to his country club and played his new and improved game.

Our minds are fascinating and most of us never tap into our full potential. Try these techniques and see how much more effective you can become.

Discover Your Family

Once again my son and I are going to embark on a grand trip together; we'll soon be seeing places of great splendor and with historical and spiritual significance. We are taking our second journey to the Middle East. We arrive in Amman, Jordan, and then from there, we'll tour Israel. We both love the opportunity to experience new people and places. More exciting, however, is the opportunity to be together, creating meaningful memories that will last a lifetime.

I can't help but think about all the things many of us in life mean to do, plan to do, but never seem to do. One of the most obvious, is spending time with our children. We have a rich opportunity every day, as we invest ourselves in our family. For people who desire achievement, it becomes a terribly easy thing to get swept up in the many demands of daily duties to the exclusion of the important obligations. To me, nothing is more important, more God-honoring, or more in my best interest, than being and investing in my family.

So, my son and I embark on our sojourn of discovery and marvel at most of them, but I'm confident that over the years, the thing we'll look back on with the greatest fondness will be the memories of those moments together when we shared a grand experience.

You see, our children need to be near us, to know us and to gain affirmation from us. In all the many little ways during all the very busy days, we must snatch opportunities and build up our relationship with our kids. To so invest is to avoid regret.

Give your children time and you'll be giving them one of the most meaningful gifts ever. You'll never achieve anything that will come close to the achievement of a family well raised.

Relax , *Enjoy!*

My son and I recently returned from our second trip to the Middle East. The first stop on our journey was Amman Jordan. We went there to visit the "Rose Red City" of Petra. The Nabateans had built this marvelous place, cut out of rock in a southern Jordan canyon and is popularly remembered as the location from the Spielberg film, *Indiana Jones and the Last Crusade.* Petra was everything we had hoped it would be and more.

Our ten-day adventure included many historical sites throughout Israel as well, and we learned a great deal for having went. The best lesson we learned was how to cope with uncontrollable circumstances. You see, we traveled to Jordan but our luggage went someplace else. So for the whole ten-day trip,, we had to wear the same clothes!

For people who desire achievement, it becomes a terribly easy thing to get swept up in the many demands of daily duties to the exclusion of the important obligations. To me, nothing is more important, more God-honoring, or more in my best interest, than being and investing in my family.

You know, in your journey for achievement, you'll have many experiences that will be beyond your ability to manage. You can get worked up with worry; you can bitterly complain; you can become distraught with grief, but the best response is to go with the flow when things are out of control.

Over the years, coping with uncontrollable circumstances has been difficult for me. I like to manage events and I don't like unmanageable surprises. Of course, I've lived long enough to know that life is full of just such surprises. I've also come to realize that you're a lot better off if you relax and accept the moment for what it is.

In our experiences we'll always have uncontrollable circumstances to contend with; the title of a popular book gives good advice, *Don't Sweat the Small Stuff (And It's All Small Stuff)*.

There was a time when I would have gone ballistic over the loss of luggage, but not this time. I wasn't happy about it, but I knew it was beyond my control and I was determined not to allow anything to detract from the enjoyment of my time with my son in this most meaningful and beautiful region of the earth.

As the others in our trip got the news of our circumstances, several offered us articles of their own clothes to see us through. We also made new friends, as people daily asked us if we'd heard about our luggage and joked about our distinct fragrance! We ended up enjoying ourselves without the burden of having to drag luggage from place to place.

You know, in your journey for achievement, you'll have many experiences that will be beyond your ability to manage. You can get worked up with worry; you can bitterly complain; you can become distraught with grief, but the best response is to go with the flow when things are out of control. By the way, when we got off the plane in Chicago, our luggage rolled off the conveyor belt. It too had traveled to the Middle East and returned no worse for wear.

What's Kissing Got to Do with It?

The subject of long life and success has attracted people for many generations. Great adventurous journeys have been undertaken to find the secret to both. The quest for the Holy Grail, Aladdin's Lamp or the Fountain of Youth have been fruitless, but now the secret can be revealed, at least for men. Fellows, can you believe it, you can literally kiss your way to the top!

A German team of psychologists, physicians and insurance companies undertook a research project to determine the secret of long life and success, and discovered that kissing your wife before you go to work can greatly increase your likelihood of longevity and success! Those who smooched their wives in the morning had fewer car accidents, missed less work due to illness and earned 20 to 30 percent more money than their non-kissing counterparts.

Researcher Dr. Arthur Szabo offers this reason for the increased benefit of kissing, "A husband who kisses his wife every morning begins the day with a positive attitude." It's great to know that something so enjoyable is good for you too!

Well, as a result of this scientific discovery, I've determined to be a man of action. From now on, I'm going to give my wife a great big kiss before leaving for work.

Here's to us babe, to long life and prosperity! Hey, it's the least I can do for the family; it'll be a pleasure.

Can't We All Get Along?

One of the most important abilities is the ability of getting along with others. The Stafford Research Institute found that the money you make in any endeavor is only 12% knowledge based; the largest percentage, 87½%, results from your ability to get along with others! Wow, pretty stunning stats!

Successful people know how to get along. The reason this is so important, is that no one can really succeed without the help of others. Consider the value notables of the past have placed on this ability:

> *"The most important single ingredient to the formula of success is knowing how to get along with people."*
>
> Theodore Roosevelt

> *"I will pay more for the ability to deal with people than any other ability under the sun."*
>
> John D. Rockefeller

> *"It doesn't make much difference how much other knowledge or experience an executive possesses; if he is unable to achieve results through people, he is worthless as an executive."*
>
> J. Paul Getty

You just can't beat getting along with others, if you want to achieve success and significance in life and business.

Fellows, can you believe it, you can literally kiss your way to the top!

John Maxwell, speaker and writer, remarked about a sign he saw in a service station while traveling in the south. It read:

Why Customers Quit
1% die
3% move away
5% other friendships
9% competitive reasons (price)
14% product dissatisfaction

But . . .
68% quit because of an attitude of
indifference toward them by some employee!

Learn to get along; treat others as you would have them treat you. Help others just for the joy of helping. When you help someone else receive what they need, there will be someone along the way that will help you.

L-O-V-E

One of the most powerful ingredients to achievement is love. Love that is evident regarding our vocation and more importantly, love for those who are intertwined in our life. You may labor long and hard and amass the many accoutrements of success; you may become famous and sail forth with a sterling reputation for success, but if you have not become immersed in love, you've very little of consequence. Two thousand years ago, Seneca made the point well: "If you wish to be loved, love."

Frederick Speakman wrote a book entitled *Love Is Something You Do*. I believe we can learn the essence of love just from Speakman's title. Love is about actions. William Wordsworth said, "That best portion of a good man's life—His little, nameless, unremembered acts of kindness and of love."

I like the remembrance of Norman M. Lobsenz. His wife became seriously ill and he felt drained of all energy and wondering what he could do. It was in the dark moments of his wife's illness, and his despair, that a memory of his childhood came to light. He recalled:

You just can't beat getting along with others, if you want to achieve success and significance in life and business.

"I was about ten years old at the time, and my mother was seriously ill. I got up in the middle of the night to get a drink of water. As I passed my parent's bedroom, I saw the light on. I looked inside. My father was sitting in a chair in his bathrobe next to my mother's bed, doing nothing. She was asleep. I rushed into the room.

'What's wrong?' I cried. 'Why aren't you asleep?' Dad soothed me. 'Nothing is wrong. I'm just watching over her.'"

Love is about actions. . . . Love gives life meaning. Without it, we truly are living valueless lives.

That recollection helped Lobsenz cope with his own situation and served to refresh him with the motivation of love.

Recently, Senator Barry Goldwater died. In tribute to him, an interview he did with Charlie Rose for CBS in 1987 was replayed. During that interview, Mr. Goldwater was asked by Charlie about regrets. The thing that caused Mr. Goldwater obvious pain was that he hadn't spent much time with his family. His wife had recently died and his children had gone on with their lives, and though he had had a remarkable career, it was the importance of love for family that had most impressed him. He admonished all to cherish their families.

Love gives life meaning. Without it, we truly are living valueless lives. Nothing is more important to cultivate. Love for God, love for family, love for all those we are in relationship with. Don't squander time for love by focusing on transitory images of success. Money, power and fame, to the exclusion of love, is a sad jail of emptiness.

Chapter Eight

Action

See It, Do It, Add to It!

You can't plow a field by turning it over in your mind. You've got to take action. You must be a doer and not just a wisher. You've got to get off your "ifs" and "buts" and do something.

You don't need to always be original to achieve. Some of the most successful people are those that take an idea someone else has had and make it work. We've all met the would-be inventors, song writers, and business starters who had a great idea but never did anything with it. What a shame. But an achiever can get a hold of something someone else only talks about and actually go out and do it.

Some years ago, Thomas Edison visited the governor of North Carolina. The governor was quite lavish in his praise of Mr. Edison's inventiveness.

Edison puzzled the Governor when he stated, "I am not a great inventor."

Perplexed, the Governor responded, "But you have over a thousand patents to your credit, haven't you?"

"Yes, but about the only invention I can really claim as absolutely original is the phonograph," Edison replied.

The Governor, now even more perplexed, said, "I'm afraid I don't understand what you mean."

Edison then went on to explain how he was able to accomplish so much. He said, "I guess I'm an awfully good sponge. I absorb ideas from every course I can, and put them to practical use. Then I improve them until they become of some value. The ideas which I use are mostly the ideas of other people who don't develop them themselves."

So, it is important to listen, look and then to do something. Don't think that only the most gifted succeed. Usually, the most gifted spend their time on ideas they don't follow through on. The victor's prize goes to the person who takes action. It's not just what you know that matters, but rather, what you do with what you know.

See the Sunny Side

I have learned optimism. While there may be many people who are optimistic by nature, I'm not one of them. I've had to learn to approach life optimistically. I could be negative and pessimistic if I wanted to, but I don't want to.

Optimism is a paradigm of hope; it sees life's setbacks as temporary, thus allowing for a come-

You must be a doer and not just a wisher.

The victor's prize goes to the person who takes action.

back. Pessimism, on the other hand, views setbacks as permanent. Pessimism lessens the likelihood of achievement. It doesn't take a rocket scientist to figure out that being optimistic is the better way to go. In fact, there is evidence that optimism is healthy for the body as well as the soul.

Dr. Daniel Mark of Duke University did a study involving over 1,719 men and women who had heart disease. The pessimists, not believing they would recover, fared worse than the optimists. Of the pessimists, 12 percent died within the first year. Only 5 percent of the optimists died! It's clearly better to have hope.

It should be noted for all you non-optimists that optimism can be learned and its benefits are documented in research done by Dr. Martin Seligman, in his book, *Learned Optimism.*

One interesting example from his study has to do with an experiment conducted with the swim team at the University of California at Berkeley. The purpose of the experiment was to reveal which swimmers were optimists and which were pessimists.

Coaches falsified the results of each heat so the swimmer was defeated, with a slower time than was actually attained. The optimists responded by swimming faster in the next heat, while the pessimists swam slower. Pretty significant effect, don't you think?

One of those Berkeley swimmers was Matt Biondi. He swam seven events at the Seoul Olympics. During the first event, though leading throughout, he slowed down and lost his lead and the heat. However, as an optimist, he determined to do better and ended up winning the next six medals!

Optimism's secret is that it produces perseverance and perseverance produces achievement. Samuel Johnson was correct when he said, "Great works are performed not by strength, but perseverance." Over the years, I've learned that an optimistic attitude enables me to try again and again until the achievement is gained.

Dream and Do

Doing the things necessary to achieve isn't always easy. In fact, most of the time, the steps to winning are tedious and tiring. You see, great accomplishments are gained through incremental progress. A little here, a little there, that's the way to success. You win if you do what it takes; if you can make yourself do the little things daily that get you where you want to go. E.M. Gray made a good point when he said,

"The successful person has the habit of doing the things that failures don't like to do. The successful person doesn't like doing them either, but his dislike is subordinated to the strength of his purpose."

Optimism's secret is that it produces perseverance and perseverance produces achievement.

Desire, passion for purpose, that's the ticket. How bad do you want to win? Will you do the little things that others won't? Will you cultivate the habits of achievement? Don't just think of the future, but think about now. Will you begin in this moment? Napoleon Hill said, "It's not what you are going to do, but it's what you are doing now that counts."

Consider the story of a 24-year-old pharmacist from Minnesota. In 1935, he visited Washington, D.C., for the first time and enthusiastically wrote a letter to his wife. It says, "I can see how someday, if you and I just apply ourselves and make up our minds to work for bigger things, we can someday live in Washington and probably be in government, politics or service. . . . Oh gosh, I hope my dream comes true—I'm going to try anyhow."

This was obviously a man with a dream, but as the letter reveals, he also was willing to do the little things over time to realize his dream. How did he do? Well, in 1946, he became mayor of Minneapolis; in 1949, he successfully ran for the U.S. Senate; in 1964, he was selected to serve as the vice-president of the United States under Lyndon B. Johnson. Hubert H. Humphry realized his dream and served in government for thirty-two years. Step by step he accomplished his dream and the good news is that you can too! So, what are you going to do today?

Decide, Then Do It

It never fails to amaze me how so many folk choose to live lives of mediocrity. They are driven, not by challenging goals, but by ease and amusement. Though they speak of dreams, they do nothing of substance to make those dreams come true. Then, they complain that they're bored and that life is so unfair.

Life pretty much consists of those things we decide to do. There are plenty of unforeseen circumstances that happen along the way, but we've been given a marvelous opportunity to shape our lives through the choices we make.

You see, great accomplishments are gained through incremental progress. A little here, a little there, that's the way to success.

Life pretty much consists of those things we decide to do.

In 1967, Newsweek Magazine printed a two-page piece entitled, "Advice To A (Bored) Young Man" in its "Responsibility Series." This is what it said:

"Died, age 20; buried, age 60. The sad epitaph of too many Americans. Mummification sets in on too many young men at an age when they should be ripping the world wide open. For example: Many people reading this page are doing so with the aid of bifocals. Inventor? B. Franklin, age 79.

The presses that printed this page were powered by electricity. One of the first harnessers? B. Franklin, age 40.

Some are reading this on the campus of one of the Ivy League Universities. Founder? B. Franklin, age 45.

Others, in a library. Who founded the first library in America? B. Franklin, age 25.

Some got their copy through the U.S. Mail. Its father? B. Franklin, age 31.

Now, think fire. Who started the first fire department, invented the lightning rod, designed a heating stove still in use today? B. Franklin, ages 31, 43, 36.

Wit. Conversationalist. Economist. Philosopher. Diplomat. Printer. Publisher. Linguist (spoke and wrote five languages). Advocate of paratroopers (from balloons) a century before the airplane was invented. All this until age 84.

And he had exactly two years of formal schooling. It's a good bet that you already have more sheer knowledge than Franklin ever had when he was your age. Perhaps you think there's no use trying to think of anything new, that everything's been done. Wrong: The simple, agrarian America of Franklin's day didn't begin to need the answers we need today. Go do something about it."

The eighty-four years of Franklin's life were spent in pursuit of achievement. How are you spending your time here?

Instead of tuning out the world, try making it better. Instead of whining about how bored you are, try getting off your excuses and do something constructive with the remainder of your life.

Instead of tuning out the world, try making it better.

If you don't like where you are in life, then do something about it. Don't stop living until you have to.

Ideas Are Important

There is one thing stronger than all the enemies in the world: and that is an idea whose time has come.

Victor Hugo

Ideas are powerful things. They carry the seeds of innovation and problem solving. They provide the necessary beginnings to great achievement. No city was ever founded and built that didn't start as an idea. No invention that brought progress and convenience would have been possible without someone having the idea. Ideas are the result of creativity and a desire to make a difference. Without them, we'd be grasping in the dark.

All of us have ideas but often feel them to be insignificant. Many times there have been people who are quick to tell us how foolish our ideas are. Criticism often stifles creativity so that we become hesitant to risk. This, of course, robs the world of what could be some wonderful ideas.

When Samuel Morse came up with the idea that electricity would carry a message across a wire, he was laughed at. Many obstacles that would've stopped most only fueled Morse to press on. He strung a wire from a hotel in Baltimore to a hotel in Washington, D.C., and a United States Senator was privileged with hearing the first message: "Behold what God hath wrought!"

So, don't allow others to steal your thunder. Having ideas and acting on them is the only way you'll know their ultimate value. Afraid of risks? Don't be. Bernard Shaw was right when he said, "A life spent making mistakes is more useful than a life spent doing nothing."

Entrepreneur; Nov. 1997, p. 8.

Stop Thinking and Go to It!

Sometimes you just can't get enough facts. If you're a cautious soul, you may be really frightened of risk when faced with an opportunity. That's understandable. You'd like to know all the pros and cons before you step out and take action. The problem, however, is that opportunity seldom comes wrapped up so neatly.

The essence of what it means to be an entrepreneur is the willingness to risk. Taking action based upon the facts and raw gut instinct, make for the seizing of opportunity.

No invention that brought progress and convenience would have been possible without someone having the idea.

The bottom line is action. Take it or lose out.

Now wait a minute. Don't bail on me here. I know what I'm conveying has a scary scent to it, but hang on a little longer.

To be successful in a venture absolutely requires as much information as possible. The more detail you can possibly nail down before embarking on a project, the better off you are.

Having said that, the ultimate test will always be a decision to jump in and go ahead. Napoleon made the point well when he said, "Take time to deliberate, but when the time for action has arrived, stop thinking and go to it."

If the facts point to disaster, then don't be foolish, but there are many times when the only way to know if something is going to work is to do it. Karl Weich said, "Chaotic action is preferable to orderly inaction. Don't just stand there, do something."

We've all known people who never attempted anything because they couldn't rule out failure. Believe me, you can do everything right, having enough information to fill many books, and still fail. So what.

The bottom line is action. Take it or lose out. Goethe said, "Thinking is easy, acting is difficult, and to put one's thoughts into action is the most difficult thing in the world." I would add to that by saying that though difficult, it is also the most crucial and beneficial.

Fear is the culprit that keeps many from going forward but I also think that laziness comes into play as well. Let's face it, risking is not only scary but it requires tremendous effort. You don't achieve anything of great value without some sweat. If I want weeds I don't have to do a thing, but if I want a beautiful garden, I'd better get busy. I think old Edison was right in saying, "The reason a lot of people do not recognize opportunity is because it usually goes around looking like work."

What is it you really want to do? What do you know about it? What is required to be successful in what you want to do? Are you willing to do what's required? The answer to the last question goes a long way in your determining the course to set out on.

So, get all the facts you can, and then, in the words of the illustrious Captain Jean Luc Picard, *Engage!*

You don't achieve anything of great value without some sweat.

Chapter Nine

Change

Change Is Inevitable: Growth Is Optional

In life you can count on one thing remaining constant: change. All that lives changes. This fundamental fact must be recognized and accepted or frustration and fear will govern. Because most people dread change, it becomes important to dispel the negative aspects of it and embrace the positive.

We don't like change because it boots us out of our comfort zone; it takes away familiar turf and thrusts us into new territory. Without change, however, we make no meaningful progression.

Change equals growth. That's the concept we need to be impressed with. Gail Shecky once wrote, "If we don't change, we don't grow. If we don't grow, we are not really living. Growth demands a temporary surrender of security. It may mean a giving up of familiar but limiting patterns, safe but unrewarding work, values no longer believed in, relationships that have lost their meaning. As Dostoevsky put it, 'taking a new step, uttering a new word, is what people fear most.' The real fear should be the opposite course."

There are so many that have become nostalgic, believing the best days are behind them. They hate the change that leaves the past behind. It has been said that our becoming nostalgic is a preparation we make for our deaths. While enjoying fond memories of days gone by is pleasurable, it should not be allowed to preclude the joy of the unexplored days to come.

The most exciting aspect of change is the potential for self-discovery and self-development. To embrace change is to prepare for growth; to cooperate with the life-stretching events that come our way each and every day we live. Change is inevitable but growth is optional. We must decide to respond positively when life changes on us.

As things happen and challenges come, learn to see them as circumstances pregnant with the possibility of personal growth. We usually don't think that way. Leo Tolstoy was right when he said, "Everyone thinks of changing the world, but no one thinks of changing himself."

Fred Smith, a noted author and leadership expert, made the following observation: "Something in human nature tempts us to stay where we're comfortable. We try to find a plateau, a resting place, where we have comfortable stress and adequate finances. Where we have comfortable

We don't like change because it boots us out of our comfort zone; it takes away familiar turf and thrusts us into new territory. Without change, however, we make no meaningful progression.

associations with people, without the intimidation of meeting new people and entering strange situations.

Of course, all of us need to plateau for a time. We climb that plateau for assimilation. But, once we've assimilated what we've learned, we climb again. It's unfortunate when we've done our last climb. When we have made our last climb, we are old, whether 40 or 80."

As the world turns, we must resist allowing our lives to become a soap opera; we must resolve to moving beyond past failures, or past successes, for that matter. As things change, don't collapse into a heap of despair or blame, but rather, determine to allow the change to become a vehicle of growth. When the bullets of change explode around your feet, start dancing.

The Customer Is Always Right

I was recently coming back from a morning appointment when I pulled into a well-known fast food place. I was hungry for breakfast: a big fat-laden (may my heart forgive me) egg, sausage and cheese croissant! I was all set to chow down on the run with one of my favorite morning fill-me-ups; I hurriedly pulled into the drivethrough jockeying to get to the speaker that would set in motion my anticipated breakfast. When I finally placed my order, the voice on the other end said, "Breakfast ends at 10:30 a.m." It was 11:00 a.m., and I had missed it! When asked what I wanted, I just said, "Never mind, thank you" and drove off.

As I made my way onto the highway, it occurred to me what had just happened. A business that literally spent millions of dollars on advertising to bring in customers, had just lost one because breakfast ends at 10:30 a.m.

Now, I understand that there are considerations behind their scheduled food offerings. Yes, I understand the logistics in food services. But, think with me for a moment. If a food business is going to capture a local market share, then should they really be telling a customer when and what to eat?

Businesses must meet the perceived needs of their customer base. This requires a resolute determination to change the system if the system doesn't satisfy the people who provide the bottom line.

Hold on, don't get all bent out of shape thinking I'm just whining about not getting my cholesterol fix. There's a larger issue here. Businesses must meet the perceived needs of their customer base. This requires a resolute determination to change the system if the system doesn't satisfy the people who provide the bottom line.

Companies are like people; they get stuck in their ways. They resist change and develop attitudes that are counter productive to their best interest. Breakfast really ends when the customer says it ends.

Companies are like people; they get stuck in their ways. They resist change and develop attitudes that are counter productive to their best interest.

All things considered, I didn't lose out. Later that day I had a heart smart lunch and am a better man for it. But the encounter, I must admit, left a bitter taste in my mouth. Not the effect a food business wants conveyed, I'm sure.

To be competitive, you have to adapt. The marketplace changes rapidly and businesses must embrace those changes to survive. As individuals, we must also adapt to change. Companies that don't, go out of business; people that don't miss countless opportunities.

I was reminded that day of this valuable principle; change or lose. I'm changing. I'm eating less fatty foods. However, I suppose that at the restaurant, breakfast still ends at 10:30 a.m.

How to Become a Valuable Employee

Everyone wants to get ahead in their career and distinguish themselves as valuable assets to the company they work for, but few apply the techniques necessary to stand out. To become a valuable employee, it's imperative to develop the kind of superior habits that makes an indelible impression on the higher-ups. In other words: you've got to stand up to stand out.

Standing up means taking the initiative in positioning yourself to be noticed. This doesn't mean trying to grandstand and take credit for everything; and it doesn't mean being a "yes-person," always telling the boss what he/she wants to hear. It does mean, however, doing the positive things that go into producing exceptional work. Here's *how* to stand up to stand out.

- **Build relationships**. Learn to get along with others. Take an interest in those around you. Discover those areas of mutual interest. Loners don't do well in work groups.

Standing up means taking the initiative in positioning yourself to be noticed.

- **Build your reputation**. Be reliable. Learn to be timely in the completing of work projects. Illustrate an ability to anticipate and meet needs.
- **Build upon your strengths**. Don't focus on your weaknesses, but learn to position yourselves on work projects that require your strengths.
- **Be technologically literate**. Get over any fear you have of the ever-changing technology. No one can expect to be highly employable without computer skills. Rather than run from it, go for it.
- **Be diligent in recording your contributions to the company**. Don't be shy about noting your achievements.
- **Network, network, network**. Make friends and influence people. Be helpful to others and you'll receive help when you need it.
- **Get in sync with your company's goals**. Companies desire employees that are team players and contribute to the overall objectives of the firm.
- **Above all else, see yourself as a unique enterprise.** In the past, you would get a job with a company and expect to have a long and prosperous relationship. Today, however, you might have many different jobs with many diverse companies. In order to prosper in today's job market, you must be in a constant state of personal and career development. It's about *You, Inc.*

Those who fail to evolve in skills are often left behind when a company decides to downsize. Making yourself a valuable employee requires concerted effort and a determination to achieve. If you're willing, you can certainly begin today doing the necessary things to put yourself in a promising position. Don't just expect to receive, be prepared to give. That's what being valuable is all about.

Decide for Yourself

Utilizing our free will is one of the most important tools we have in constructing a successful life. Our wills, when exercised for success, pave the way of winning in life. Likewise, we can use our wills to self-destruct.

Sheriff Ralph Jones of LaFayette, Georgia, had a profound effect upon one of country music's greatest legends. Johnny Cash was touring and had stopped overnight in LaFayette.

Cash had started using amphetamines as well as other substances in order to stay energetic while on tour. His choice of this solution caused his marriage to break up and he began to miss concerts and get arrested because of his behavior as a result of alcohol and drugs.

Such was the case in LaFayette, Georgia. Sheriff Ralph Jones arrested Cash and locked him up.

The next morning, Sheriff Jones released Cash and gave him back his pills. What he said to Johnny would become the catalyst for change in Cash's life. He said, "I've watched you on television and listened to you on the radio; we've got your albums of hymns. We're probably the two best fans you ever had. It broke my heart when they brought you in here last night. I left the jail and went home to my wife and told her I had just locked up Johnny Cash. I almost wanted to resign and just walk out because it was such a heartbreaking thing for me. Here, take your pills and get out of here. Do with your life whatever you want to. Just remember, you've got the free will to either kill yourself or save your life."

That plain, straight talking sheriff told Cash just what he needed to hear. He spent the next month withdrawing from the drugs and alcohol. He had help, but he couldn't have done it without choosing for himself.

If you're not pleased with your situation in life, then make a decision to change. While it may be in vogue to blame circumstances or other people for the life we now have, the fact is, we are today the sum total of the decisions we've made during our yesterdays. Exercise your will and begin to succeed.

It All Depends on How You Look at It

"It all depends on how you look at it!" I can't count the number of times I've heard that line. But you know, it's true. So much of life's opportunities have to do with how we look at them. One person's crisis is another person's opportunity.

How we see things is called a paradigm. Some years ago, when Mickey Mantle was 61 years old, he was approached by a 45-year-old fan and his son. The man, obviously excited, said to his little boy, "Son, it took me 30 years to get here and

If you're not pleased with your situation in life, then make a decision to change.

The way we look at things can help us or hinder us when it comes to being effective and successful in life.

shake this man's hand. This is the greatest baseball player who ever lived." The man's son looked at Mantle and then looked at his father and said, "Daddy, that's an old man." The man and the boy's paradigm were different when it came to Mickey Mantle.

The way we look at things can help us or hinder us when it comes to being effective and successful in life. Many businesses have failed largely due to the way those in those businesses choose to view the changing world around them.

The Swiss, for more than a century, were noted for their fine craftsmanship in the watch industry. In 1968, they dominated 65% of the world's market and 80% of the profits. In 1967, Swiss researchers invented the quartz watch but the established Swiss watch industry wasn't interested; they weren't open to new ways of doing things. They just couldn't see it. After all, it had no gears or springs. So, they didn't even bother to protect their invention!

The Japanese on the other hand, weren't closed to the idea. They could see the possibilities. So they began production and in ten short years became dominant around the world in watch making. The result devastated the Swiss watch industry. In the seventies and early eighties, over 50,000 of the 65,000 watch workers had to be laid off in Switzerland. All because they couldn't see the possibilities. They had a paradigm problem.

"It all depends upon how you look at it!" Are you open minded in the way you see opportunity? Are you able to see what could be, instead of referring to what has always been? Are you the kind of person that sees beyond the obvious; who can visualize what others can't even imagine? If so, you have a good shot at real achievement. No matter what, don't stop looking!

Why Not Try It?

It's amazing how being confronted with a challenge can motivate us to attempt great endeavors. The achiever, that is, the person who doesn't let setbacks hold him/her back, responds to challenge as a personal invitation to succeed. Such was the case of Clarence Sanders.

In 1916, Clarence Sanders owned a family grocery store. Though he had worked long and hard, nothing seemed to make a difference. His business was failing. One day while walking to a cafeteria for lunch, he passed the local bank. The moment he passed by, the banker ran out to encourage him. "I've been going over your books, Clarence," the banker called out. "It looks to me like you've got about three more months before you're going to be bankrupt. Have a nice lunch!" Some encouragement, huh!

Clarence walked on to the cafeteria with a lot going through his mind. As he stood in the line that seemed to stand still at times, a thought occurred to him. If people were so willing to stand in line just so they would have the opportunity to serve themselves, why not try that in the grocery store business?

Sanders went back to his store and quickly went to work converting it to a self-serve grocery. He renamed the new store employing this radical concept, "Piggly-Wiggly." It became the first modern-day supermarket! In 1923, Sanders sold his business for twelve million dollars.

Challenge is the way the achiever views what others refer to as a hopeless situation. Of course, it takes work to tackle such projects as those fraught with difficulties. Vidal Sasson was right when he said, "The only place that success comes before work is in the dictionary." So, it's important to have the right attitude, as Clarence Sanders did, when being challenged by life. You've got to believe in yourself. If you don't, who else will?

Challenge is a magnet for achievers. Don't be repelled by it, let it draw you. I love the story of Ernest Shackleton. He believed that if he presented a challenge to people, they would positively respond.

Shackleton wanted to lead an expedition to discover the South Pole. It would be difficult at best and he needed a strong crew of men that would dare to do what many felt impossible. He decided to put the following ad in The Times of London:

> "Men wanted for hazardous journey. Low wages, bitter cold, long hours of complete darkness. Safe return doubtful. Honor and recognition in the event of success.
>
> E. Shackleton"

The next morning, over 5,000 men responded! In 1907, Shackleton was able to reach the South Pole. People do respond to challenge. Inherent in every challenge is the seed of greatness.

If you lead people, don't be afraid to challenge them. If you're presently faced with a challenge, don't be afraid to tackle it. Remember the words of that great comedian, W.C. Fields, "...a dead fish can float downstream, but it takes a live one to swim upstream."

Challenge is a magnet for achievers. Don't be repelled by it, let it draw you.

10 Chapter Ten

Purpose

The Ripple Effect

I like walking bridges that span small ponds. Why? Well, they're good places to think. One of my favorite things to do while standing on a bridge is to drop small stones into the water. I like to watch the ripples. OK, it may seem like I desperately need to get a life, but I find this simple act relaxing and insightful.

It seems to me that the immensity of human life is symbolized by the pond, and our individual lives, by the small stones dropped. All stones when dropped in the pond, make ripples. All lives have influence. The choices we make ripple through the immensity of human life and generations are impacted.

Sometimes we're tempted to think that the way we live and the choices we make, are our business alone and matter to no one else. We may even feel that our lives don't count. Like **George Bailey** in *It's a Wonderful Life*, we wish we were never born.

The simple pristine truth is that we are here for a reason and our lives do count. We have this great ability to determine the kind of ripples we'll make in life; to live now in such a way that future generations can benefit.

Consider the true story of two men and the ripples of their lives. Max Jukes was an atheist and married to a woman who was also an atheist. Their union produced 310 who died as paupers, 150 who were criminals, 7 who were murderers, 100 who were drunkards. Half of the women were prostitutes. Max Jukes' 540 descendants ended up costing the state a quarter of a million dollars.

Another man, Jonathan Edwards, a contemporary of Max Jukes, was a devout Christian man and he married a woman of faith. Their union produced 1,394 known descendants. Among that number were 13 college presidents, 65 college professors, 3 United States senators, 30 judges, 100 lawyers, 60 physicians, 75 army and navy officers, 100 preachers and missionaries, 60 authors of prominence, one a vice-president of the United States, 80 public officials, 295 college graduates. There were governors of states and ministers to foreign countries as well. His descendants didn't cost the state a dime.

Yes, that we live is important; but *how* we live is even more important. While it may be true that I need to get out more, I do think I'm on to something here.

The simple pristine truth is that we are here for a reason and our lives do count.

Sometimes You Have Only One String in Life

"I studied the lives of great men and famous women, and I found that the men and women who got to the top were those who did the jobs they had in hand, with everything they had of energy and enthusiam and hard work."

Harry S. Truman

There is something wonderful in the lives of those who are driven by a passion for achievement. They possess the ability to be propelled forward, out from among the mediocrity of the pack. They are able to do what others are baffled by and refuse to allow the obstacles that trip most, to slow them down.

Niccolo Paganini was a great violinist. His father had given him violin lessons while he was very young. At the age of nine, he made his first public appearance that launched him to fame throughout Europe. His skill was applauded as genius and he was especially revered for his ability to push the violin beyond what had previously been the accepted boundaries.

During one of his concerts, the audience sat spell-bound at Paganini's brilliant mastery. As he played, it seemed that time stood still. The crowd was breathlessly riveted to each note, awaiting the next, when suddenly a string on his violin broke. Paganini kept playing. Suddenly, a second string broke; he played on. Amazed, the crowd didn't know quite how to respond. When the third string broke, leaving Paganini with one string to finish with, the crowd jumped to their feet, applauding his great passion and skill with all their might. Truly this was a wonderful genius at work!

The powerful passion of his life made the difference when obstacles presented themselves to his path. Many would quit, he played on.

When faced with life, determine to have a passion. Don't allow yourself to be embraced by the hand of mediocrity. Choose to discover what really excites you and gives you a sense of joy in facing the day. Play at life like Paganini!

When faced with life, determine to have a passion. Don't allow yourself to be embraced by the hand of mediocrity.

Chapter Eleven

11

Knowledge

Know It All!

As a professional speaker, I'm often asked to make presentations before groups of business professionals. The trick in being a successful professional in the speaking industry is knowing your subject, knowing your audience and knowing when to shut up!

The first key is knowing your subject. Alexander Gregg once said, "Get into your subject. Get your subject into you. Get your subject into your audience."

People want to know that you know what you're talking about if they're going to spend the time listening. Good speakers listen to, read and devour information. They are keen observers. This allows them to *know their subject.*

The second successful key a professional speaker needs to know is the audience. People are different from one another, and groups of people are different as well. Good presentations are audience specific. When you are asked to speak before a group, find out as much about them as possible.

Any insight you can gain can be of help. What will be the average age of the audience member? Predominant gender in attendance, political leanings, economic brackets, or any other pertinent information that can help you develop a presentation sure to communicate.

The third key is knowing when to shut up. Always leave people wanting more when you're speaking. Sometimes verbosity can hurt you in fact. Consider that George Washington's inaugural address, the shortest on record, was only 135 words.

On the other hand, William H. Harrison's inaugural address was 9,000 words long and took two hours to deliver! On the day he spoke there was a freezing northeast wind that made the lengthy speech seem even longer than it was. President Harrison paid dearly for not knowing when to shut up. He came down with a cold and died a month later from pneumonia!

So to be effective as a speaker, know your subject, know your audience and know when to shut up. Hey, it works for me!

The trick in being a successful professional in the speaking industry is knowing your subject, knowing your audience and knowing when to shut up!